"That's a lot of bread and  *on at one time."*

"But that's what I wa   are down.

She finally took a st   der on her pad. "Then that's what you'll get, Abe Glick, along with a big spike in your blood sugar to go with your clogged arteries."

"Are you saying you're worried about my health?" He had to force himself not to show his amusement.

"No, of course not. I was just calling it to your attention, that's all. If you want to go to an early grave, who am I to stop you?"

He blew out a breath. "Then what do you suggest I have?"

"It's not my place to suggest what you should have. If you want—"

"Tell you what, Mary. I'll change my order if you'll consider going out with me after work."

"Why?"

"Because I want to get to know you better. I like you, Mary Penner."

DEBBY MAYNE has been a freelance writer all her adult life, starting with slice-of-life stories in small newspapers, then moving on to parenting articles for regional publications and fiction stories for women and girls. She has been involved in all aspects of publishing from the creative side, to editing a national health magazine, to freelance proofreading for several book publishers. Her belief that all blessings come from the Lord has given her great comfort during trying times and gratitude for when she is rewarded for her efforts.

Books by Debby Mayne

Shades
of the Past

Debby Mayne

Heartsong Presents

This book is dedicated to my daughters, Lauren and Alison, and my granddaughter, Emma.

Thanks to Lee Miller and Pastor Rocky Miller for answering dozens of questions about the Mennonite community in Sarasota.

I appreciate Tara Randel's willingness to read the first few chapters and the suggestions she made to help bring this story to life.

A note from the Author:
I love to hear from my readers! You may correspond with me by writing:

Debby Mayne
Author Relations
PO Box 721
Uhrichsville, OH 44683

ISBN 978-1-61626-331-7

SHADES OF THE PAST

Our mission is to publish and distribute inspirational products offering exceptional value and biblical encouragement to the masses.

PRINTED IN THE U.S.A.

one

Mary Penner lowered herself to the hot, moist sand, gathered the front of her skirt, and twisted it around her shins as she pulled her knees to her chest. She carefully tucked the folds of her skirt around her to cover herself. It was only May, yet the intensity of heat from the sun reflecting off the beach in Sarasota, Florida, sent droplets of perspiration trickling down her back. But she didn't mind. Being here in a stable home, living among the Conservative Mennonite folks, and knowing her grandparents would always be there for her gave her a sense of peace—even if they wished she'd never been born.

Mary still had confusing and sometimes even bitter moments when she couldn't put her past completely behind her. Today was especially difficult because it was the ninth anniversary of her mother's death.

The gentle whisper of waves as they lapped the sand blended with the sound of seabirds on their never-ending search for food. Children scampered around blankets, sand buckets in hand. Teenagers and young adults lay sprawled on beach towels, catching the last of the day's rays, their bronze bodies showing very little modesty. Years ago she would have been among them, but now. . .well, it embarrassed her.

Mary extended her arm and studied her shadow before she pointed her index finger and drew a figure eight in the slightly moist sand. That was how her life seemed sometimes—a double circle that started out as though going someplace, yet it managed to meet back up at the beginning. Just like her thoughts.

"Mary?"

She snapped her head around at the sound of the familiar voice. "Oh hi, Abe."

He drew closer and squatted. "Nice day."

"Yeah." Mary sniffled and turned slightly away from Abe Glick. His presence had always created the strangest sensation—sort of a dread mixed with exhilaration in her chest. The stirrings of emotion confused her as always. "What are you doing here?"

Abe chuckled. "I was about to ask you the same thing." He gestured to the sand beside her. "Mind if I join you?"

She cast a quick glance in his direction, then looked back toward the water, hoping he wouldn't notice her heat-tinged cheeks. "That's fine."

He slowly sat down and stretched his long, navy-blue twill-clad legs toward the water. "It's a mite hot today."

"I don't mind."

A Frisbee zoomed a few feet past them, followed by a half-dressed teenage boy. "Sorry," he said. His gaze lingered long enough to satisfy his curiosity, then he took off after the Frisbee.

Abe nodded toward the kid, a half smile on his face, before turning to face Mary. "So what are you thinking about?" Abe asked.

Mary shrugged. "Work. Family." She paused to take a deep breath before adding, "Just everyday stuff."

"I don't think so." Abe tilted his head back and let out a deep chuckle. "Based on the look on your face, I think it's much more than that."

Mary darted a quick look in his direction, then turned back toward the water. "Is it any of your business?"

He lifted his hands. "Sorry if I offended you, but I did it innocently, I promise."

His apology deflated her short burst. "That's okay. I'm sort of touchy today anyway."

"So do you wanna talk about it?"

Mary snorted and shook her head. "You are something else, Abe. Do you ever give up?"

"Giving up isn't in the Glick vocabulary."

"Okay, so what if I tell you I was thinking about the past?" Mary leveled him with an I-dare-you-to-ask-more-questions look. "Does that make you happy?"

He looked right back at her with as much of a dare as she had. "Ever miss your old life?"

"Never." She paused as she considered his question. "I love being with Grandma and Grandpa. They're good to me."

"Indeed they are." Abe's sidelong glance at her heightened her pulse rate. "There was never any question about that." He turned completely toward her and stared until she met his gaze. "Or was there?"

He asked too many questions, and she was growing more irritated by the second. "No, of course not!"

"You don't have to be so defensive, Mary. I'm not the enemy."

A soft grunt escaped her throat. "Never said you were, Abe. What's this all about anyway?"

"Just curious, I s'pose."

"Curious? How about nosy?" Mary shifted a few inches away from him. "Why did you follow me all the way here?"

"Who says I followed you?" He lifted an eyebrow and gave her a teasing grin.

Mary mimicked his expression, then turned back to face the water. "Did you have some business on the beach?"

"Ya, I came to see you."

"See? That's what I'm talking about."

Abe laughed. "You're too easy to rile, Mary Penner."

"Is that what you're trying to do? Rile me?"

His teasing had always annoyed her.

He lifted a shoulder then let it drop. "Maybe."

"Stop trying to make me mad, Abe Glick," she tossed right back. "Sometimes it seems like that's all you live for."

"Oh there's much more to life than making you mad, Mary. I like making you laugh and getting you to think. And sometimes it's fun to scare you. Remember that snake?"

"How could I forget that snake? That *fake* snake. You got me in so much trouble, you're lucky I'm talking to you now."

"I don't believe in luck." He gave her a teasing grin. "Sounds like you're holding a grudge."

"Maybe I am."

Abe touched Mary's arm. "That was eight years ago, so if you aren't over it by now, I would suggest you start working on not holding grudges. God doesn't want us to be angry."

"That was seven years ago," she corrected, "and I'm not angry."

Abe snorted and turned to face the water. "Sure is pretty, isn't it? I can't imagine living in a place where I couldn't get to the beach once in a while."

"No one ever asked you to."

"You're still a mite touchy, Mary. I suppose I should leave you to your thoughts."

"Excellent idea."

"If you ever wanna talk about anything, I'm a good listener." He touched her arm. "I promise not to judge your past."

Mary swallowed hard and nodded. "I'll remember that."

Abe stood and brushed most of the sand off his backside. A small amount of the wet sand still clung to his trousers. "I best be getting back to the farm before the sun goes down."

She lifted a hand for a brief wave, then waited until he was out of sight before getting up. Her midshin-length skirt held more sand than Abe's trousers, but it never bothered her until Grandma fussed at her for tracking it into their tiny rented home in the Pinecraft community. She shoved her feet into the tan clogs she'd worn to work. The sand was still gritty on her feet, and it irritated her until she left the beach, took them off, and carefully brushed the tops and bottoms of her feet. She clapped her shoes together and put them back on. Other people darted past her, some of them openly staring and others trying hard not to. She'd gotten used to being noticed for wearing plain clothes, but when she'd first arrived in Sarasota, she felt awkward. Some of the Mennonites set themselves apart from the Amish by wearing brighter colors. Grandma still clung to her Amish roots, but Mary didn't mind. Her brown skirt and off-white blouse helped keep her from being noticed, which was just fine with her. Her *kapp* covered about half her head and tended to fall to one side in spite of the pins she used to secure it.

As Mary walked to the bus stop, she thought about Abe's offer of lending an ear. She'd been in Sarasota for a little more than nine years, and to this day, no one had discussed her past—at least not with her. Abe had come close a few times, but he never pressed for information, and she never offered it. They'd never actually talked much beyond the teasing and gentle jousting that he always started.

She'd always thought her teenage crush on Abe would fade, but sitting next to him on the beach proved that wasn't the case. If things had been simpler, Mary might have given in to her feelings. The anniversary of her mother's violent death continued to remind her she'd never be like other Mennonites, who'd all led godly lives since birth.

When Mary first arrived in Sarasota, she remembered the fear of facing Grandma and Grandpa after hearing all the stories from Mama about how they'd shunned her when she got pregnant out of wedlock. Her story shifted slightly with each telling, but the pain in Mama's voice was evident every time; that part never changed. Even if Mama embellished her story,

Mary couldn't doubt there was a foundation of truth to what she said had happened.

As difficult as Mama had made their lives, Mary still missed her. Mama was loving and kind to Mary. She said she'd do anything to make things better, but she'd gotten herself into so much trouble, she didn't know how to dig her way out. Mary had to guess what Mama was talking about, but it wasn't too difficult to put the pieces together. The love was there, but without guidance or a parenting role model, Mama made some terrible mistakes—including one that had cost her life. Mary leaned against a light pole and squeezed her eyes shut as the memory of that awful night pounded through her head.

The wind shifted slightly, bringing her back to the moment. Mary blinked as the bus pulled to the curb, the fumes surrounding her and making her cough.

"Hey, lady, are you getting on or not?" The bus driver leaned toward her as he waited with his hand on the door crank.

"Oh. . .sure." Mary gathered her skirt up and climbed onto the bus. She found a seat near the front and plopped down then stared out the window. Mary was on her way to Grandma and Grandpa's house, just like nine years ago, only now she knew her place. Her memories had always transported her somewhere she didn't want to go, and sometimes she couldn't keep the demons away. If Mama had told her more about her father, she might have had someone else to turn to. The times Mary had asked about him brought such sadness to Mama, she eventually gave up and created an image in her own mind of who he might be. When she was little, she pictured a prince riding in on a stallion, but as she got older, his image darkened, and he became a brooding man similar to those in Mama's life.

Mary had been puzzled the first time she met the people Mama said had shunned her. They'd both embraced her and told her she was one of them now—and she had nothing to worry about as long as she followed God's Word and His calling to be a good Mennonite girl. There were a few people who weren't as open, but Grandpa reminded her that no one was perfect. Occasionally Grandma would mutter something about having another chance at raising a daughter—only this time they wouldn't make the same mistakes.

৯

Abe arrived at the old family farm in time to send his hired workers home and finish putting away some of the tools for the day. His grandfather had resisted the transition from farming celery to dairy farming and growing citrus, but after Grandpop passed away, Abe had managed to make the changes when he returned from college, where he got his business degree. Dad was pleased with Abe's work, and he retired from farming after Mom died. He had moved into the Pinecraft community in town so he could live among other Conservative Mennonites.

A grin played on Abe's lips as he reflected on the last time he'd visited Dad in town. He'd been on the shuffleboard court and didn't seem to want to be interrupted. If Abe didn't know better, he'd think Dad preferred his new life over what he'd done the first almost fifty years of his life. Although Dad had once loved farming, the combination of all the heavy lifting and the hot Florida sun had taken its toll on him. Abe still did some of the farmwork, but he'd managed to put what he'd learned about business management into practice and hired some workers to do most of the manual labor. Abe's job was to manage the farm and find ways for it to sustain itself and the people who depended on it. After a shaky year, the farm was in good enough financial shape to pay everyone, including Dad, a nice wage after expenses.

Once the last of the equipment was put away in the new barn Abe had built, he brushed off his trousers and headed into the old house that he now lived in alone. The echo of the screen door slamming reminded him of how lonely it had gotten since Dad moved out. Both of his brothers had their own places—Jake on a neighboring farm and Luke in a swanky neighborhood in Sarasota. Jake was more like Abe; he had no desire to go crazy during *rumspringa*, the one-year running-around period some of the Mennonite families carried over from their Amish ancestors. However, once Luke got a taste of worldliness, he didn't want to go back. While some families would have shunned their children, Dad never did that to Luke. Dad didn't like Luke's choices, and he'd taken every opportunity to let him know it, but he still embraced his wayward son. Abe reflected on Dad's decision and determined he would have done the same thing.

Mary's grandparents, according to the bits and pieces he'd heard, had made the traditional choice when their only daughter, Elizabeth, had gotten pregnant during her rumspringa. They'd shunned her. Although he'd just been born when it happened, he'd heard about it from the Conservative Mennonite children when Mary showed up at school. Parents used her and others who experienced something similar to remind their children how worldly allure wasn't all it was cracked up to be.

Abe had heard about the Penners' shame and how they mourned the loss of their daughter for years. In fact, until Mary came to live with them, they seemed like very bitter people. The only contact he'd had with them when he was a child had been when he went into their restaurant with his folks. He'd never seen a smile touch their lips before Mary arrived.

The very thought of Mary made him warm inside. The first time he'd seen her when she arrived at their tiny school had sent his heart racing. He laughed to himself as he remembered how difficult it had been for her to adjust to the

Mennonite ways. She grumbled about everything—from the head covering she couldn't seem to keep straight to the skirt that constantly got twisted between her legs. She questioned authority and balked at some of the conservative teachings in the early years. The few times she spoke, she went for shock value and blurted things the other Mennonite kids had never heard about before. But he suspected there was more truth than fiction in her words. Dad had told him he heard that a drug dealer killed her mother when he suspected she was about to turn him in.

It didn't take Mary long to clam up and withdraw. Most of the other girls ignored her, and the boys were a little afraid to go near her. Abe wasn't scared of much, including Mary, so he teased her every chance he got. Her reactions were more exciting than any of the other girls' would have been, and he found her scrappiness intriguing. As a teenager, he didn't know any other way of showing how much he liked her.

Abe shuddered at the thought of what Mary must have seen as a child. When he was at college and learned about the evils of the world, he'd developed a keen sense of the difference between right and wrong. Mary needed a friend, and he resolved to be just that. He'd thought about Mary during college, and when he met other girls, he couldn't help but compare them to her.

He'd been stopping by Penner's Restaurant when he came to town, and each time he saw Mary, he did whatever he could to get her attention. The chemistry between them was powerful—stronger than all the common sense in Sarasota. He couldn't put together an intelligent sentence the first time she asked for his order. When she laughed at his feeble attempt, he relished the sound of her laughter. He'd had to go home and practice talking to her before going back the next day. This had gone on for more than a week before he was able to formulate a plan.

Abe had wanted to see Mary when he first came back from college, but there was so much work on the farm, he had wanted to square that away first. He'd been back from college about eight months when he first walked back into Penner's Restaurant and spotted Mary. He was struck hard by how much she'd matured.

If things worked out, maybe he and Mary could be more than friends. He'd always thought her differences made her special.

☙

"Mary? Is that you?" Grandma's voice echoed through the tiny, sparsely furnished house. She appeared by the main room, her scowl dredging up a sense of shame in Mary. "Where did you go? Your grandpa said you left the restaurant early."

"The beach." Mary was on her way to the bedroom when Grandma stepped in front of her, arms folded, her heavy eyebrows arched. "Oh no, you don't. I'll not have you tracking sand in this house after all the time I spent cleaning up today. Back outside." She jabbed a finger toward the door to drive her point harder.

Mary did as she was told. During the time she'd been with Grandma and Grandpa, she'd learned the ropes, but today her thoughts had shoved common sense to the back of her mind. She'd managed to shake off most of the sand, but Grandma took the broom to her skirt and loosened the grains that had gotten stuck in the seams and folds.

"Now go on inside and wash up and help me get dinner on the table. Your grandpa will be back soon, and I don't want to make him wait."

As soon as she stepped back inside, a sweet aroma wafted from Grandma's kitchen. She turned to her grandmother. "Peanut butter pie?"

"Ya. That's for dessert, and only if you do as you're told."

Mary sighed. She was twenty-three, yet she was still treated as a child. She'd offered to move out, but Grandma and Grandpa told her no, not under any circumstances. They said she needed them to look after her until she found a suitable husband to take care of her. Where they expected her to find someone who'd want to marry her was beyond Mary. Besides, after what she'd seen, she knew the only decent man under God's sun was Grandpa.

Grandma's expression remained stoic as she handed Mary a short stack of stoneware plates to set on the table. The two of them worked in silence, giving Mary's mind another chance to wander. Even after all these years, Mary remembered how her mother hated a quiet room so much she'd turn on a television just to drown out the silence. The quiet didn't bother Mary all that much, but she did rather enjoy hearing something besides the clatter of dishes, forks, and spoons. But her grandparents went along with the traditional Mennonite ways of not listening to music or watching TV. The only concessions they made were some of the conveniences that came with the house they rented.

By the time Grandpa walked in the back door, everything was ready. He sat down and without a word reached for her and Grandma's hands. As he said the blessing for their food, Mary thought about his humble words. "Lord, thank You for giving us this home, this food, and one another. I pray that You continue to keep us on our narrow path until we reach the gates of Your righteousness. Bless our souls, and thank You for this day. Amen."

Normally Mary would have been starving and eager to dig into Grandma's specialty meat loaf. The salt air from the beach should have given her enough of an appetite to eat, but she wasn't hungry. She'd been busy at the restaurant, and as had happened many times, she'd forgotten to eat lunch.

"Well, are you going to answer your grandpa or not?"

Mary blinked and looked back and forth between her grandparents. "I'm sorry, Grandpa, but I missed what you said."

A tiny flicker of a smile tweaked his lips. "Abe was looking for you after you left the restaurant. Did he find you?"

"Yes." Mary looked down at her plate and swallowed hard before looking back at Grandpa. "He found me at the beach."

Grandpa pushed his chair back and tilted his head as he quietly regarded Mary for a few seconds. "Ya, I told him he might find you there."

"You never told me you were with Abe," Grandma said. "I've taught you that withholding information is the same as lying."

Mary wanted to explain that she'd gone to the beach alone and left alone, but she knew it wouldn't matter. "I'm sorry, Grandma."

"Sarah," Grandpa said softly. His forehead crinkled as he shook his head at Grandma then turned back to Mary. "How long were you and Abe at the beach?"

"I was there about an hour. Abe came after I got there, and he left long before I did."

"She wasn't with Abe, Sarah. She wasn't lying. He went looking for her, and it sounds to me like she didn't give him the time of day."

Grandma shook her head and stood, grabbing her plate and Grandpa's to carry to the sink. "You'll never find a husband if you keep treating all the nice men like that."

Mary was confused. First Grandma seemed upset about her being with Abe, and now she wanted her to be nice to him. Her stomach churned, and the peanut butter pie Grandma had made didn't sound so good. Mama's angry words played in the back of her mind as she thought about how nothing she did around here seemed to be good enough. Sometimes Grandma seemed halfway happy, but Mary still hadn't figured out what it took to get a lasting smile from her. When she smiled, it was unexpected, and it flickered but quickly vanished. Mary knew Grandma loved her, but she was obviously afraid to show it.

"May I be excused?" Mary asked.

Grandma had her back to her, but she slowly turned. "I made this pie 'specially for you, Mary. Don't tell me you don't want it."

"She'll have some," Grandpa said as he stood up and walked around the table. "Just give her a few minutes for her food to settle. Why don't the two of you ladies take a break? I'll clean up the kitchen."

"I'll not have you cl—" Grandma began.

Grandpa shushed her by placing his hands on her shoulders and turning her toward the door. "I said I'll clean up. Why don't you two take a stroll around the block, and by the time you get back, I should be all done."

The last thing Mary wanted to do was be alone with Grandma, but she was too tired to argue. She looked at Grandpa, who winked and made a shooing gesture.

As soon as they got outside, Grandma started talking. "Your grandpa thinks I'm too hard on you. He's afraid you'll run off like your mother did. Is that going to happen?"

Mary allowed a few seconds to slip by before speaking. "No. I don't plan to leave."

"Neither did your mother." Grandma's voice cracked.

Mary was sick of being compared to her mother. "I'm not my mother." The instant those words left her mouth, she regretted how harsh she sounded. "I—"

"Ya. Thank the Lord."

"My mother was good to me."

"Maybe so, but look how she left you." Grandma slowed down. "Today is the anniversary of—"

"I know."

"I've been thinking about her all day. It isn't easy, you know, raising a child up in the Lord, only to have her turn on me like she did."

"She didn't mean to hurt you, Grandma."

"But she did. Very much. I may never get over it."

"Mama did what she thought she had to do." Mary cleared her throat. "I've never understood what happened, though. She tried to tell me, but some things didn't make sense."

"Do you want me to tell you?"

"Yes." Mary knew Grandma's story would likely be quite different from Mama's, but this was the first time she'd ever offered to discuss it. Grandma had obviously been doing the same thing Mary had all day—thinking about Mama. "I'm ready to hear the truth."

Grandma stopped and squeezed her eyes shut. A tear trickled down her cheek as her lips moved in silent prayer. When she opened her eyes, Mary saw the pain etched in them.

"I'm sorry, Grandma. If it hurts too much, you don't have to talk about it."

"Neh, it's time you heard the truth." Grandma paused long enough to gather her thoughts before she began. "She wanted to go stay with some friends she met at the restaurant, in spite of my worries," Grandma began. She coughed and sniffled.

"She told me about those friends, and they didn't seem so bad."

"Those girls were horrible, and they taught her how to be disrespectful to her faith."

"I'm sorry, Grandma, I didn't mean—"

Grandma held up her hand to shush her. "Your grandpa and I have been talking about this quite a bit lately. He thinks I should tell you everything. I guess today is as good as any to do that."

"I would like to know more," Mary said softly. Mama

had told her all about how Grandma had flown into a rage, telling her to leave and never show her face again.

"I'm ready to tell you our side of it." Grandma hung her head as she reached for Mary's hand. Mary's shock sent a lump to her throat. "I love you, sweet girl. Just like I loved your mother. She hurt us more than you'll ever know—unless you have a daughter of your own who storms out and never returns."

Mary swallowed hard. "But I thought—"

"Be quiet and let me tell you."

Mary forced herself to nod. She knew Mama had been hurt, and her perception had been tainted by her childish anger. After all, Mama was only sixteen when she left home. But Mary also knew Grandma's memories were slanted from her perspective—just like Mama's were. "Okay, please tell me."

Grandma pulled a tissue from her pocket and dabbed at her eyes before she opened up. "These girls were here on vacation—down from Cincinnati. Elizabeth met them when they came into the restaurant looking for something to do. Her plain clothes and different ways fascinated them, so they invited her along everywhere they went."

Mary smiled. She understood how those girls must have felt because when she first arrived in Sarasota, she'd been awestruck by the plain lifestyle.

"I didn't want her to go, but your grandpa said it would be good for her. After they left, I was relieved, but only for a short while because after they went home, they sent word that they wanted her to visit them up in Cincinnati. She'd obviously told them about rumspringa, and they wanted to show her their way of life. Again, your grandpa said we should let her go. Besides, he pointed out that she planned to leave town, and it would be nice to know she had a place to stay, so off she went. When she came back, I knew she was different. Four months later, it was obvious she'd never be the same." Grandma slowed her pace and rubbed her abdomen. "She was pregnant with you. I said some things. . ."

"I know," Mary said. "Mama told me."

"I couldn't help it. When I had my rumspringa, things were very different."

Mary smiled. "What did you do during your rumspringa?"

"Helga and I went to town and bought some lipstick. Then we went to a dance party that she heard about from some boys. The second we walked into that place, we knew it wasn't good for us, so we left."

Mary couldn't picture her grandmother wearing lipstick, and showing up at a dance party? That was unfathomable. She laughed. "Were you and Helga by yourselves?"

Grandma's stern lips turned up at the corners, and she finally allowed herself a full grin. "Ya, but we didn't leave that party alone."

"Grandma!" Mary couldn't hold back her shock. "Did you meet some boys there?"

"We knew a couple of them, ya. But don't get so alarmed. One of them was your grandpa. He and Paul got there right before we arrived, and they didn't like it any more than we did. So they offered to take us home."

It must have been scandalous at the time, but everything obviously worked out fine, since Grandma and Grandpa were still married and Helga was still married to Paul. They lived in Pinecraft, just two blocks away from the Penners. Paul had a small candy store not far from the community with a corner nook featuring Helga's crafts.

"I think your grandpa should be done with the kitchen chores by now. We need to get on back."

"Grandma, before we go any farther, I want to know something."

"Just ask me, Mary. Don't drag it out."

"If you had it to do over again with Mama, would you have done anything different?"

Grandma's soft expression instantly returned to a scowl. "It never does anyone any good to have regrets. It's too late to look back and say what I should have done, so I won't even think about it like that."

two

Abe pulled out his cell phone and punched in the number of his favorite ride into town. It was too difficult in this modern world to drive a horse and buggy. Accidents on the highway left many of the Mennonites and Amish dead or with debilitating injuries, so he relied on the services of folks who made their living transporting those who didn't drive cars.

David answered right away. "Sure thing. I can be there in fifteen minutes."

"That'll be just fine." Abe finished getting ready, then went out to wait on the front porch.

The large white van pulled into the shell-encrusted driveway exactly fifteen minutes later. "Where to, Abe?" David asked as Abe slid into the van.

"Penner's."

David chuckled as he pulled out onto the road. "That Penner's place must have some great food for you to go there every day."

"Not every day," Abe reminded him. "They're closed on Sundays."

Abe saw the look of amusement on David's face, but at least the man had the decency not to continue this train of thought. "How's the farm doing? I can't help but notice the changes. Seems like there's something different every time I come out here."

"Ya, I've made a few changes in the last year."

"Things must be going well then."

"Can't complain. We work hard, though."

"So when do you think you'll need some more workers? I have a couple friends who are out of work."

"Out of work? Why?" Abe folded his arms and stared out the window as they whizzed past alternating farms and patches of palmettos.

David shrugged. "Layoffs. The economy's been rough lately."

"So I've heard." Abe could use another worker or two, but they had to be able to jump right in without much supervision. "Any of your friends have farming experience?"

"Probably not."

"Can't use 'em then."

"How about you meet them first, before you make a decision? I can't speak for all my buddies, but I think a couple of them would be good at farming if they knew what to do. They're hard workers, too."

Abe pondered that thought for a moment before crisply nodding. "I s'pose that would only be fair. I've already asked around the Mennonite community, and no one else is beating my door down for a job."

"Thanks, Abe. I'll send my friends your way. Is it okay if they call your cell phone?"

"Of course. How else would they get hold of me?"

"True." David snickered. "I bet you're a tough man to work for."

"No. Just fair. I expect people to earn their wages, and I pay them what they're worth."

"Interesting concept," David said. "Too bad more people aren't like you."

Abe slowly shook his head. "That might not be such a good thing. God created us all different for a reason."

"Good point." David pulled into the Penner's parking lot. "Want me to pick you up here at a certain time, or should I wait to hear from you?"

"I'll call," Abe said as he got out of the van. He handed David some cash. "Thank you for the ride, David. See you later."

David waved before he took off. Abe turned around and faced the front of Penner's. For a moment, his resolution to work his way into Mary Penner's life wavered, but he recognized his fear of rejection and dismissed it. That should never keep a man from following the Lord's plan for him, and he was fairly certain of what God wanted. Otherwise, why would God plant Mary's image on his brain so indelibly?

"Abe." Joseph Penner greeted him at the door. "Good to see you again. Where would you like to sit?"

Abe nodded toward the right. "Is Mary still working in that section?"

Joseph grinned. "She's supposed to be in the kitchen this morning, but I can send her out if you want to see her."

"Neh, don't change things on account of me." Disappointment flowed from his chest to his abdomen, but he tried his best not to show it. "I'm sure we'll see each other again soon."

"Go find a seat that suits you, Abe, and I'll have someone right over to take your order. Want coffee?"

"That would be good."

Abe had only been seated a few seconds when Mary showed up. Even dressed in plain clothes, she glowed with a unique beauty—with her deep green eyes and peaches-and-cream complexion framed by strawberry blond hair that peeked out from beneath her traditional head covering. A stray wisp hung down over her forehead, but she didn't seem to notice it.

"Grandpa said you wanted to see me?" She lifted an order pad and poised her pen above it. "Do you know what you want yet?"

Abe didn't have to look at the menu; he knew it by heart. "I'll have a tall stack of pancakes, sausage links, two fried eggs sunny-side up, fried potatoes, and a side order of buttered toast."

"Pancakes and buttered toast?" she asked. "And all that fried food?"

"Ya, that's what I said."

She licked her lips and grimaced. "That's a lot of bread and grease for one person at one time."

"But that's what I want." Abe challenged her with a stare down.

She finally took a step back, nodded, and jotted his order on her pad. "Then that's what you'll get, Abe Glick, along with a big spike in your blood sugar to go with your clogged arteries."

"Are you saying you're worried about my health?" He had to force himself not to show his amusement.

"No, of course not. I was just calling it to your attention, that's all. If you want to go to an early grave, who am I to stop you?"

He blew out a breath. "Then what do you suggest I have?"

"It's not my place to suggest what you should have. If you want—"

"Tell you what, Mary. I'll change my order if you'll consider going out with me after work."

"Why?"

"Because I want to get to know you better. I like you, Mary Penner."

Her arms fell to her sides, and her pen fell and rolled across the floor. "What?"

"I would like to take you somewhere." It was hard not to laugh.

Mary narrowed her eyes in suspicion. "Where?"

Abe bent over to retrieve her pen as he tried hard to think

of someplace specific, but nothing came to mind, so he relied on what he knew she enjoyed. "You like the beach, so why don't we go there?" He held out the pen.

She grabbed the pen from his hand. "I went to the beach yesterday."

"Then maybe out for ice cream?"

She remained standing there, her stare intense, the surprise still evident on her face. "What is this all about, Abe? Did Grandma or Grandpa put you up to something?"

"Are you saying you don't trust me? Or your grandparents?"

"No, of course I'm not saying that. I just want to know why you're suddenly tracking me down, following me everywhere I go."

Abe leaned back and regarded her before saying, "I don't follow you everywhere."

"Okay, so what do you call what you did yesterday when I was at the beach? And now?"

"The beach isn't everywhere."

Mary made a low growling sound. "You know what I mean."

"What is wrong with wanting to get to know you better?"

"Nothing, except you should know me well enough after all these years."

Abe tried to tamp down the hurt. "You make it sound like torture."

One corner of her mouth quirked into a grin. "Well, sometimes it seems that way."

He lifted his hands in defeat then let them fall, slapping the table. "Okay, okay, I can tell when I'm getting the brush-off. I'll leave you alone. Now if you'll please bring me my breakfast, I can be on my way sooner rather than later."

Mary turned slightly, then glanced at him over her shoulder with a coquettish look, her cheeks a little rosier than normal. "Grandpa will probably let me leave at three o'clock when the new server comes in, if you'd like to come around then. Maybe a walk on the beach would do us both some good."

ॐ

Abe's reaction was priceless. His chin dropped, and his eyebrows shot up. As Mary headed back to the kitchen, she had the sensation of floating a few inches above the floor. Grandpa did a double take as she passed him, but he didn't say a word. However, she did hear a soft chuckle, letting her know he was aware that something was up.

Ever since she spotted Abe in the corner of the classroom when she first arrived, Mary thought he was cute. He'd obviously noticed her, too, but not in the same way. From the moment they exchanged their first words, he seemed bent on tormenting her with practical jokes and mild, good-natured taunting. He was funny, but she worked hard not to let him know she thought so. And he hadn't changed much.

Not wanting to face Abe so soon after her emotional vault, Mary talked Shelley, one of the other servers, into bringing him his food and the message that she'd see him at three o'clock sharp out in front of the restaurant.

Shelley came back, laughing. "He was definitely disappointed to see me, but he said to let you know he'll be there on the dot."

"Good," Mary replied. "I don't like it when people are late."

"That's because you're a Penner. Your grandparents insist on punctuality, which is why there are so few of us working here."

"I'm sure." Mary also knew that the small staff had something to do with her grandparents' frugality. They didn't believe in having more than what was needed, including employees. Grandpa expected everyone to work hard, but he compensated everyone well enough to keep the conscientious people.

"So are you and Abe dating?" Shelley asked.

"Ha. Not in this lifetime."

Shelley stood still and cast a questioning glance Mary's way. "You said that awfully fast." She folded her arms and narrowed her eyes as a sly grin worked its way to her lips. "That usually means something."

Mary planted a hand on her hip and scowled. "It means nothing, except if I don't agree to go out with Abe Glick, he'll keep after me until I do, so I might as well get it over with."

"Then what?" Shelley smiled.

Mary lifted her hands. "Then we go right back to how we've always been."

"Which is?"

"Do you ever stop asking questions?"

"Okay," Shelley relented, turning back to pick up the next order. "I guess it's none of my business."

"I guess you're right." Shelley started to walk away. "Wait, Shelley."

Shelley turned around, the plates balanced on her arms. "Ya?"

"I—I just wanted to tell you how much I appreciate you trying to help."

"You really need to think about opening up and letting people in a little more."

Mary forced a smile and nodded. Shelley would never understand. Whenever people looked at Mary, she was sure they saw her mother—and in this community, that wasn't a good thing. Other people had left, and she heard the talk.

The rest of the day was busy as always. Between visits from the Mennonites and Amish from the Pinecraft community and the tourists, Penner's Restaurant did quite well. Grandma's pies were especially popular. Folks from other parts of the country had heard of her peanut butter, pumpkin custard, banana cream, and key lime pies, and once they tried them, they spread the word even more.

Around two thirty, Shelley pointed to the clock. "A half hour to go. Do you need to freshen up? If you do, I'll cover for you."

"No, I'm fine." Mary thought about how disheveled she must look after serving the busy lunch crowd. "It's just Abe."

"Abe is a very nice-looking man."

"You think so?" Mary asked. "Then why don't you go for him?"

Shelley let out a low growling sound. "You're impossible, Mary. You know I already have a man."

"But you're not married or engaged."

"Not yet," Shelley conceded. "But I have a feeling it won't be long." She tilted her head and batted her eyelashes. "And now it's your turn to find love."

"I think not. There is no one around here who would even consider getting engaged to me." Shelley was one of the few people who'd given her the time of day since they first met, so she'd understand. "People can't seem to separate me from my mother."

"That's not true. I think you're the one who can't let go of what happened. A man who has a heart for God understands what a good woman you are and what an excellent wife you will make. If I'm reading him correctly, Abe wants to court you."

"Maybe you need stronger glasses, Shelley." She wiped her hands on the dishrag and tossed it onto the counter. "I think I will go check my kapp. I wouldn't want any loose hair flying around."

"Oh no, you wouldn't want that," Shelley teased. "Heaven forbid Abe would see your hair down."

"Quite frankly," Mary admitted, "I don't care one way or another, but Grandma and Grandpa do care, and I'm not about to get them mad."

A minute later, Mary stood in front of the restroom mirror, kapp in hand, studying her hair. Her mother had always said it was her best feature, but according to Conservative Mennonite custom, she wasn't allowed to show it off. Or at least not all of it.

She removed the clip, raked her fingers through her waist-length hair, then wound it back up in a bun and refastened it. She tucked in her kapp on the sides to expose a little more of her hair before pinning it back into place. Her makeup-free face was pale from being indoors all day, so she pinched her cheeks to give them a little color. Not that she cared what Abe thought. She just wanted to freshen up a bit.

Once she was satisfied with how she looked, she tried to scoot out of the restaurant but stopped when she heard her name. "Mary, it's not three o'clock yet. Where are you going?"

Mary turned around to face Grandpa, who stood there with a knowing smile. "Um. . .I don't want to be late."

"Eager to see Abe, are we?" He was obviously working hard to hold back his laughter. "Never mind. I'm sure he's just as excited to see you."

"I am not eager or excited to see Abe."

"Of course you're not." He flicked his hand toward the door. "Go on, get out of here. You and Abe have some fun, okay? Tell him I said so."

"I will, Grandpa." Mary left without arguing. Grandpa was too old to understand anything on her mind, so there was no purpose in telling him.

⁂

Abe had arrived a few minutes early. In his haste to be on time, he had David pick him up at two o'clock.

"Got a date?" David said.

"In a way, I suppose it is. Why?"

"Twice to town in one day. I'm getting used to daily, but

there's definitely something going on."

"Nothing going on but getting to know a smart-mouthed woman who makes me laugh."

David tilted his head back and guffawed. "That's the best kind. You'll never be bored if she can make you laugh."

"Neh, I'd never be bored with her, that's for sure."

"So, does she like you, too?"

"Ya, I can see it in her eyes, but she doesn't know it yet. She keeps trying to put me in my place, but that won't work with me."

"Looks to me like it's working." David had turned the music down on his radio, but the sound of the bass still thumped through the van. He tapped his steering wheel in time to the music as Abe thought about what David had said.

"How you figure?" Abe finally asked.

"Figure what? That whatever she's doing is working on you?"

"Ya."

"You keep coming back for more."

Abe scrunched his face. "Never thought about it that way."

"You don't have much experience with women, do you?"

"Neh, I've spent most of my life studying and learning about the farm."

David nodded. "That's what I figured. You're a smart man, Abe. If you ever want some pointers, I'll be glad to give you some."

"No offense to you, David, but I'll try to figure her out on my own. You never met anyone like Mary Penner."

"I'm sure. If she's got you all worked up, she must be quite a woman."

Abe folded his arms and tucked his hands under his arms as he snickered. "That's one way to describe her."

Mary Penner was a smart girl. After she settled down

and accepted the Mennonite ways, she was one of the best students in class. In their last year of high school, he'd asked her if she was going to college. As she shook her head no and replied that her grandparents wanted her to help with their restaurant, he could see her sadness. Mary could have done whatever she wanted, but she was loyal to the people who had taken her in. Abe admired and respected her even more for that.

As David turned the corner, Abe caught sight of Mary standing outside the restaurant. His pulse pounded through his body, and a lump formed in his throat.

"Is that her?"

"Ya." He unfolded his arms and gripped the armrest.

"Don't be nervous, man. When a woman waits for a man, it means she likes him."

Abe nodded. "That is what I'm thinking. Now I need to find a way to make her see that." He cleared his throat. "Can you slow down a bit?"

David snorted. "Don't worry, you'll be just fine. Want me to pick the two of you up later?" He pulled to a stop about ten feet from the curb where Mary stood.

"Can you wait here? We want to go to the beach, and I think we might need a ride."

"Okay." David gestured toward Mary. "You better go, or you might lose her before you have her. I'll be right here."

Abe got out and strode over to Mary, who quickly glanced away. "Been waiting long?"

She turned back to face him, her face flushed and her hands in a tight clasp in front of her. "Yup. Too long. What were you and that man talking about?"

"That's David. He's one of the folks who picks up some of the farmers when we need to come to town. He wanted to know when to pick us up."

She tilted her head and smirked. "Is that all?"

"I don't know." Abe rubbed the back of his neck with one hand and extended the other hand toward the van. "Come on, Mary. David can take us to the beach."

She hesitated. "I don't know David."

"But I do. The beach is too far to walk."

"I generally ride a bus that has a route and other people."

"I've been using David as a driver for a long time, and I trust him." He gave her the best assuring look he could. "Why would we ride the bus when David's right here?" Abe glanced over his shoulder and saw the amused expression on David's face. He didn't know what to do, so he just stood there, looking back and forth between Mary and David.

"Oh all right," Mary finally said as she forged ahead toward the van. "I'll have you to protect me if anything happens."

Abe opened the door for Mary; then he climbed in after her. "Mary, this is my friend David."

"Nice to meet you, Mary." David nodded to Mary and grinned at Abe. "Buckle up, and we'll be on our way."

They were at the beach ten minutes later. Abe helped Mary out of the van and handed David some money.

"What time do you want me to pick you up? The wife has plans for us tonight, so I'll need to be home by seven."

"We won't be that late. I'll call you."

"My evening will just be getting started." David gestured toward Mary. "See you two soon."

Abe and Mary stood on the sidewalk and watched David drive off before Abe turned toward her. "David is a good man."

"Yes, he seems to be." Mary shielded her eyes from the western sun. "There sure are a lot of people out today."

"That's because it's nice out." Abe wasn't sure what to do next, so he reached for her hand and placed it in the crook of his arm. "Let's enjoy ourselves this afternoon, okay?" For a moment, he thought she might remove her hand, but when she didn't right away, he relaxed a little.

They took a few steps on the sidewalk, then stopped to remove their shoes. It was easier for Mary because all she wore was a pair of clogs. Abe had to remove his shoes and socks, then turned to Mary in time to see the grin form on her lips.

"So what is this all about?" she asked once they resumed walking on the sidewalk beside the road. "Why have you been so adamant about hanging around me lately?"

"I—" Abe was interrupted by the honking of a horn.

"Hey, Abe! What are you doing with her? Taking a walk on the wild side?"

"Who was that?" Mary asked.

Abe narrowed his eyes and gritted his teeth. "That's Jeremiah Yoder."

"Oh yeah, I remember him. I heard he left the church."

"He did," Abe replied. "He never came back after his rumspringa."

"That happens to a lot of people, doesn't it?"

"Ya. I s'pose once some folks get a taste of the wild life, some of them have trouble finding pleasure in plain, simple living." He shrugged. "But I think most have the sense to come back." As soon as those words left his mouth, he regretted it. Abe never wanted Mary to think he was judging her for something she had no control over.

"Yeah, it must be hard." Her voice was laced with pain and defensiveness.

Abe stopped and turned Mary around to face him. "I am so sorry, Mary. I never should have said that."

"No big deal. Don't worry about it."

three

Mary tried her best to hide the lump in her throat. What Abe just described was exactly what had happened to her mother.

He continued shaking his head. "I would never want to say mean things to you, even when you aren't nice to me. I understand—"

She reached up and gently touched his lips. "Don't."

Before she had a chance to retract her hand, he reached for her wrist and held her fingers to his lips. Her heart hammered as he kissed her fingertips, one by one, until her knees almost buckled beneath her.

Abe's expression was tender as he looked down at her. Mary's dry mouth prevented her from speaking at first. She yanked her hand back and covered it with her other hand.

"I'm sorry, Mary." He grimaced then shook his head. "No, I'm not. I take that back. I'm not sorry in the least."

Mary managed to find her voice. "So what was that all about, Abe? Were you trying to distract me? Or are you in cahoots with Jeremiah and his buddies?"

"No. Never. I have nothing to do with Jeremiah."

"I don't think that's so good either." Mary shoved her fist on her hip and leaned away from Abe.

"What? Did I say something wrong?"

"So you believe in shunning people who leave the church?"

"Don't be so touchy, Mary." Abe widened his eyes as he took a step closer to her. Before she had a chance to react, he reached out and closed his fingers around her wrist again. "I never said that I believe in shunning. What I do believe in is doing what is right and standing up for someone I care about. I can't let someone say such things about you, Mary." He bent his elbow toward her and placed her hand back in the crook of his arm where it had been. "Come on. We're supposed to be walking on the beach, and that's what I intend to do."

Mary's confusion deepened. She wanted to appreciate Abe's chivalry, but she still didn't know why he'd bother with her when there were plenty of other Mennonite girls who would love to be with him.

"What's on your mind?" he asked as they stepped off the sidewalk onto the warm sand.

"What makes you think anything is on my mind?"

Abe rubbed her knuckles with his other hand. "That's my girl. I like when you answer my questions with a question of your own."

She paused at his comment, *That's my girl.* "But why?"

He beamed down at her. "You make me think. I like to be with people who make me think."

"Sometimes thinking is overrated." She stumbled over some uneven sand, and he quickly reached around to steady her. "I can be so clumsy."

"It may be overrated to you, but it keeps our minds sharp. And you are not clumsy—just a little unsteady, having trouble navigating the sand today."

Yeah, she was unsteady, but it had nothing to do with the sand. It was all about the butterflies flapping around in her abdomen every time Abe touched her or looked at her with those light brown eyes with golden flecks that sparkled in the late-afternoon sun.

They walked about a quarter mile before Abe tugged on Mary. "Let's take a break. I want to slow down and enjoy our time together." He tucked his fingers beneath her chin and tilted her face up.

Her stomach lurched, and she stepped back. Another tender moment would send her senses to a place she wasn't ready to go. She had to change the mood—quickly. "There's something else I don't understand, Abe. You went away to college and got your degree in business. What do you plan to do with your education?"

He shrugged. "I s'pose I'm doing it."

"Working on the farm? You didn't have to go to college to do that. You could go into business if you wanted to."

"What business?"

"Banking?" She couldn't think of anything else.

"Neh, not banking. I like farming. Besides, who says I'm not in business? I run one of the biggest and most productive dairy farms on the west coast of Florida. I've managed to convert the last of the celery crops to citrus, and we expect to have our best yield next season."

Mary was impressed, but her insides still swirled from Abe's nearness, making it difficult to hold an intelligent conversation. She extended her foot and glided it across the sand, smoothing out a section.

"Do you want to walk some more or sit down for a while?" he asked.

"Um. . .I didn't bring anything to sit on."

Abe laughed. "That didn't stop you before. You sat right down on the sand."

Yeah, but she didn't have anything to risk. . .like her heart. "This is a nicer skirt than the one I wore yesterday."

"Ya, I s'pose you should think about your skirt." Abe held her gaze as a suppressed grin twitched the corners of his lips.

She swatted at him. "Let's walk."

"Ouch." He feigned being injured. "Apparently you didn't know we Mennonites are opposed to violence."

"If that hurt, you're a bigger sissy than I ever thought, Abe."

He pulled his straw hat down a little in the front. "No one ever calls Abe Glick a sissy."

Mary tossed him a playful glance then took off running. "Sissy, sissy, sissy! Abe Glick is a sissy!"

"Oh, you." He ran after her and quickly caught her in his arms.

As he pulled her close, she knew running had been a big mistake. Abe had never been one to back away from a challenge, and he'd never let her get away. It took him about two seconds to catch her in his strong arms, but his grip was very gentle. He was stubborn but not mean. His Mennonite heritage ran deep with Abe—all the way to his core.

When Abe turned her around, everything outside their bubble of closeness was blurry. She wanted him to kiss her, but she wasn't ready to put herself in such a vulnerable position. A memory of her mother being fondled by one of the many faceless men in her life flashed through her mind. Panic overrode her desire, so she yanked away and nearly threw herself onto the sand as she popped out of his grip.

"What happened, Mary?" The look of concern on Abe's face tweaked her heart. "Did I hurt you?"

"No," she said quickly. "Yes, but not like you think."

"Why do you talk in circles? Either I hurt you, or I didn't. I asked a direct question, and I expect a direct answer."

"Too bad." Mary tucked the loose strands of hair back beneath her kapp. "I don't have any answers to give."

"Why do you continue to shut people out, Mary?"

"I'm not the one shutting people out. In case you haven't figured it out, other people have already made up their minds about me, and there's nothing I can do to change them."

"Maybe you're imagining some of it."

"I don't think so." She folded her arms.

He glanced at her arms then looked her in the eye. "Perhaps people are afraid to get close to you because you are so standoffish. Perhaps your shame made you that way?"

"What? I am not standoffish." She unfolded her arms and lifted her hands. "I'm as open as the next person."

He gave her a lopsided grin. "Oh you are, are you?"

"Never mind. You'd have to be me to understand." She took a step back.

His once-rigid shoulders sagged. "You confuse me."

Not as much as she confused herself. All she knew was how the flood of emotion when she was around Abe rendered her incapable of logical thinking. She opened her mouth to respond, but she had no idea what to tell him, so she shook her head and lifted her hands before letting them fall back to her sides, slapping her skirt.

They studied each other for a moment before Mary looked down at the sand. Abe took a few steps toward the water, his hands in his pockets, his hat tipped low in front. She had a brief flashback to what Jeremiah had hollered as he drove past them honking. Did Abe really like her, or did he have an ulterior motive in wanting to be with her?

She remembered Mama saying once that everyone wanted something. Was Abe looking to take a "walk on the wild side," as Jeremiah had so crudely put it? Or did Abe feel sorry for her? These were questions she had to ask herself, and she'd never be satisfied until she knew the answers.

"Abe?" She squared her shoulders and tried to put on a brave front.

He spun around and took a couple of steps toward her. "Ya?"

Mary licked her parched lips. As he looked into her eyes, her bravery faded. She offered a closed-mouth grin. "Never mind."

Abe awkwardly offered his arm, but she pretended not to notice. He quickly retracted. "Ready to head back now?"

"Yeah." Mary turned to face the water before adding, "You should call David now."

"That's exactly what I'm about to do."

Mary heard Abe let David know they were ready for him to come pick them up. After he flipped his cell phone shut, she remained standing with her back to him.

"If I knew what I did wrong, I could apologize."

"You did nothing wrong. Where is David picking us up?"

"Where he dropped us off," Abe replied. "He said he'll be there in fifteen minutes."

"Then we best get going."

Since they hadn't gone far, they were able to saunter back. Quite a few people—most of them tourists—stared at them. Mary thought she was used to it, but now it bothered her. She didn't like feeling like a sideshow. She wanted to be accepted for who she was deep down—not for something she was trying to be. The problem was that she wasn't sure who she was.

David was waiting for them when they arrived. "Glad you finished up early. The wife called and said to come home as early as possible."

"It's always a good idea to make the wife happy," Abe said as he helped Mary into the van.

David chuckled. "That's a wise comment coming from a single man."

This discussion made Mary very uncomfortable. After buckling her seat belt, she shifted and faced the window. Abe left the seat next to her empty, and he took the one by the opposite window. She didn't want to admit it, even to herself, but she enjoyed having him close. His quiet strength gave her a sense that nothing bad could happen.

Instead of chatting, David turned up the music a little louder. The oldies song on the radio brought her back to a time she constantly tried to forget. Good thing they didn't have far to go.

The van slowed down a few feet from the walkway to the

restaurant. "Nice meeting you, Mary."

She smiled and nodded. "Thank you."

"Could you wait here a minute while I walk Mary inside?" Abe asked.

David glanced at his watch then nodded. "Take your time. I don't think a few minutes will make that much difference since you called so early."

Mary got out and turned to face Abe. "You don't have to walk me inside. I know the way."

"But I want—"

"No, I'm perfectly capable of taking care of myself." She realized her tone was harsher than she intended, but she didn't feel like apologizing. Seemed lately she spent a lot of time explaining herself, and she was getting tired of it.

"Yes, I'm sure you can, Mary, and you may have your way this time." He tilted her head up to face him. "But remember that I don't give up easily."

Mary turned her back and walked toward the restaurant, knowing Abe watched her. As soon as she was inside, she heard the van door slam. Grandpa stood there waiting, but he didn't say a word. All he did was nod as she breezed past to get her things.

She started to go out the back door to her three-wheeler, but then she decided to go ahead and get the discussion over with. She put her tote on the counter and plodded toward the front of the restaurant.

"We had a very nice time at the beach, Grandpa," she said.

"Good." He grinned and widened his stance. "So will you be going out with Abe again soon?"

"I doubt it."

A frown replaced his smile. "Did he say anything inappropriate?"

"No, Grandpa. We're just both very busy people with not enough time."

"Don't say that, Granddaughter. You have to make time for what is important in life. What are you, twenty-two?"

"Twenty-three," she corrected.

"Old enough to fall in love, get married, and have children of your own."

"I'm not ready for anything that serious, Grandpa. I'm comfortable living with you and Grandma, and working here makes me very happy. I get to serve people who appreciate it."

"Ya. And you are very good at it. But this isn't what your life should be about. The Lord blesses two people who fall in love, and that's what I want for you."

Who said anything about love? "Thank you, Grandpa. Maybe someday."

"Ya, someday." He nodded. "Maybe soon."

"I'm going home to help Grandma with supper. See you at the house in a little while."

"Ya. Eleanor can close the restaurant. Tell your grandmother I'm bringing home some pie for dessert so she won't make more."

Mary left out the back door, grabbing her tote off the counter on her way out. She tossed it into the basket and hopped on her three-wheeler.

❧

David didn't say much as they rode to the Glick farm. He apparently sensed that Abe needed some quiet time. However, right before they turned onto the long shell road leading to the house, he spoke up.

"So how was your walk on the beach with Mary?"

"It was good."

They hit a bump as they turned, so David slowed down. "Don't wanna talk about it, huh?"

"There's nothing much to say."

"Is this a relationship that may lead to something bigger?"

"Bigger? Are you asking if there's romance?"

With one of his customary chuckles, David nodded. "Yeah, I guess that's what I'm asking."

Abe inhaled deeply then slowly exhaled. "That's what I would like, but I'm not so sure about Mary. She seems to still be hurting from her past."

"I take it you know something about her past that would bother her."

"Ya, but mostly what I've heard from other people, and that was a long time ago. She can't seem to let go of her past, and she thinks other people are holding it against her. I have to tread very lightly on that subject when I'm with her."

"How long have you known this girl?"

"Nine years. I met her when she arrived to live with her grandparents. She wasn't Mennonite before coming here. Her first day of school, she walked in looking so lost and scared." Abe's heart twisted at the memory. "She wore plain clothes, but everyone could tell she was uncomfortable in them, especially her kapp. She kept fidgeting with it."

"I can understand someone having a tough time getting used to the customs," David said. "No offense meant, though. All I'm saying is change is tough for most people."

"No offense taken. Ya, I'm used to this, but I can see how someone who was never around the plain and simple way of life might be uncomfortable. But that's not what bothered me."

"Obviously, something did bother you." David pulled to a stop in front of Abe's house. "Wanna talk about it? I have a little time."

"I thought you were in a hurry."

"I can spare a few minutes."

Abe pondered discussing something so personal with someone outside the faith and decided it had some advantages in this case. "Ya. I would like to talk."

David turned off the ignition and turned around to face

Abe. "So tell me what's on your mind."

"Most of the other girls didn't understand all she'd been through. All they knew was what they'd heard, and they didn't give her much of a chance. There was one girl, though, who tried to help her. That's Shelley, who works for her grandfather at the restaurant."

"Did the other girls make fun of her or say mean things?"

"Neh." Abe shook his head and leaned against the door. "It might have been easier if they had. They didn't say much of anything to her. I imagine Mary felt like an outcast."

"How about you? Did you talk to her?"

"Ya. Mary and I became friends."

"Friends, huh?" David nodded. "That's how my wife and I started out, until I got the nerve to tell her how I really felt. I was so in love with that girl, I never knew which way was up."

"I know what you mean," Abe said. "I've felt that way around Mary since before I went off to college. I thought I would forget about her, but when I came back and saw her working for her grandfather, it felt like my world got brighter." He cast his gaze downward. "I just don't know what to do next."

"Sounds like the real thing to me, Abe. So what's stopping you from just coming right out and telling her what you told me?"

"It isn't that easy. She's very touchy about getting close. I think she still has problems trusting people."

"That's understandable, after the reception you said she got when she came here."

"I think it's even deeper than that. Something happened in her past that she has never told me about."

"Do you know this for a fact?"

"Neh, but I sense it. I can imagine how she feels about people ignoring her, but she shuts me out when anything comes up about what happened before she came to Sarasota."

"Why do you care so much?" David asked. "It's not like there aren't more than enough Mennonite girls to go around."

Abe's lips twitched into a smile. He'd heard this before from his father, who kept after him to find a wife when he first returned from college. "I don't want just any girl. She has to be special."

David nodded his understanding. "I getcha, and I agree. You deserve someone special."

"I don't know about deserve. I'm happy with whatever the Lord provides, but I can't help but think He brought Mary into my life for a reason."

David's forehead crinkled, and he grew silent for a few seconds before he asked, "Any way you can find out what's bugging her?"

Abe thought for a moment, then shook his head. "I don't know." He opened the door and got out. "Thank you for listening. Have fun with your wife tonight."

David lifted his hand in a wave. "I intend to. Take care, Abe."

After Abe went inside, he fixed himself a grilled cheese and ham sandwich to keep his stomach from rumbling later. If David had more time, Abe would have ordered something from Penner's, where the food was filling and delicious.

If he hadn't set his mind and heart on winning Mary over, he could be married by now, and dinner would be a feast, no matter what she prepared. Like David had said, there were plenty of unmarried girls who would be happy to find a husband with land and a good future.

❧

"Mary Penner, you haven't said more than five words since you got home." Grandma stood at Mary's bedroom door glaring at her. "You can at least tell me what you and Abe talked about."

"We didn't say much, Grandma. We mostly just walked on the beach and looked at the water."

"Did he tell you why he asked you out on a date?"

Mary stiffened. "It wasn't a date."

"In my book, when a man asks a woman to go somewhere with him, it's a date. What do you call it then?"

"Just a walk on the beach."

Grandma placed her hands on her wide hips, closed her eyes, and slowly turned her head from side to side before looking directly at Mary. "Walking on the beach with a man is the same as going out to eat with a man. Either one is a date. What's wrong with you, Granddaughter?"

The same sensation she'd always felt when her mother used to shame her into conceding flooded Mary. "Nothing is wrong with me, Grandma. I don't know what all this fuss is about me going to the beach with Abe."

Grandma lifted a finger and shook it. "I tell you what's wrong, Mary. You're a woman now. A twenty-three-year-old woman who should start considering her future. Abe obviously cares enough about you to go out of his way to be with you."

Mary pursed her lips. Nothing she could say would make a difference in what her grandparents thought.

"Mark my words, Granddaughter, Abe is not going to wait around for you forever. I just happen to know several young women who think he would make a good husband."

Mary gasped. "I'm not even thinking about getting married."

"Maybe it's time you started thinking about it. I don't want you to become a lonely old woman with no one to love you. Your grandpa and I are all you have. If we could have had more children, you would have aunts, uncles, and cousins. As it is, after we're gone there will be no one left but you."

"Yes, Grandma, I realize that. But you and Grandpa are

very healthy, and I expect the two of you to be around for a very long time."

"Only the Lord knows, Mary. Just remember that."

Yes, and only the Lord knew what Mary should do. Now if He'd only find a way to let her know how to handle Grandma and Grandpa's nudges toward what she wasn't sure of. She'd seen plenty of successful relationships since being in Sarasota, but images of the past her mother had tried unsuccessfully to shelter her from continued to haunt her.

"I made some beef stew, and it will be ready when your grandpa comes home from the restaurant."

"I'll help you get it on the table," Mary said. "Just let me know when."

After Grandma left, Mary bowed her head and prayed. *Lord, I am so confused. I like Abe very much, and he makes me feel things no one else does. But does that mean I should do something different from what I'm doing? I want to do Your will, but I don't know what that is.* She opened her eyes then slammed them shut again. *I don't want Abe to feel sorry for me or pity my past. I do care for him, but not enough to complicate his life or mine. I would be such a burden to him, and I would never feel worthy of his name.*

Mary repositioned the kapp on her head and carefully pinned it to prevent more hair from escaping. It was almost summer, when the Florida humidity created stray frizz that would form a halo around her face. After she pulled herself together, she went to the kitchen to help Grandma get dinner on the table. Grandpa walked in with a big smile on his face.

"After you left, I heard from some people who saw you and Abe this afternoon." He turned to Grandma. "I suspect we might be planning a wedding soon."

"According to our granddaughter, that isn't likely."

Grandpa cut his glance back and forth between Mary and

Grandma and finally settled on Mary. "Then you best not be cavorting with Abe anymore, or you risk ruining your reputation."

Grandma spun around and faced Mary. "Cavorting? What did you and Abe do?"

four

Mary was temporarily tongue-tied. Grandpa plopped down in his chair and picked up his fork. "It isn't a good idea to show affection for someone in such a public place, Mary."

"Grandpa, I didn't do anything wrong. Abe and I walked on the beach. H–he took my hand and—"

"You don't need to make excuses," Grandma said. "If you did something wrong, the Lord knows about it. If not, then you have nothing to worry about or explain."

With her emotional stirrings already creating confusion, Mary couldn't argue. She tightened her lips and nodded.

Grandpa motioned for them to join him at the table. "I believe she knows what the Lord wants, Sarah. We need to trust our Mary. She's a good girl."

Although Mary was happy Grandpa defended her, he was the one who'd started this to begin with. Mama's words kept ringing in her ears. *Men can't be trusted. They only come around when they want something.*

"Mary?" Grandpa tilted his head forward and lifted his eyebrows. "The blessing."

Grandpa took her hand, gave Mary's fingers an extra gentle squeeze, and winked at her. She forced a smile and lowered her head. As he said the blessing, she tried to push Abe's image from her mind—but it was impossible.

As soon as they filled their plates, Grandpa started talking about how busy they'd been with the summer crowd lately. "It's starting early this year. I'd planned to add more to my food orders in another month, but it looks like I need to do it this week."

"I can stay later in the afternoons," Grandma offered.

"That would be good." Grandpa turned to face Mary. "Anyone you knew in school who might need a job?"

Mary slowly shook her head as she wondered why he'd even bother to ask. Both Grandma and Grandpa knew that very few of the people she knew in school would give her more than a few passing words.

"Ya, I didn't think so." Grandpa took a bite of his yeast roll and chewed as he thought about it. "Perhaps we can ask some people at church tomorrow. Eleanor is working out very well, but it's difficult for her to manage the kitchen while she's on the floor taking orders."

"Good idea," Grandma said. "This is potluck Sunday, so we'll be there longer."

Mary always felt out of place at the church potluck, and she dreaded the second Sunday of every month. After the service everyone gathered outside, unless it was too hot or rainy. Then they'd meet in the fellowship hall instead. No one was outright mean to Mary. In fact, some of the older members were very polite, but the people her age had maintained their old habit of ignoring her.

Abe had been to a couple of the dinners since he'd been back from college. She wondered if he'd be there tomorrow. A sliver of hope was dashed by dread at the thought of Grandma's eagle eyes watching her talk to Abe, waiting to pounce if she stepped the slightest bit out of line.

After dinner Mary told her grandparents that she could clean up the kitchen alone. "It's your turn to go for a walk with Grandma," she said to Grandpa.

He laughed and rubbed his belly. "Ya, that's probably a good idea after such a hearty meal."

As soon as they left the house, Mary scurried around the kitchen, washing dishes and cleaning all the counters and the table. She wanted to be done with all the work when they got back.

Abe got up early and made sure all the cows were fed before going back inside to get ready for church. One of his workers had set up a table at the farmer's market in town yesterday, and he'd left the money by the back door. Abe was pleased by the fact that everything had sold. This looked like it would be a busy tourist season, which he thanked the Lord for after hearing about the past two seasons being so lean.

He intended to go to the potluck after church with the hope of talking to Mary. So far his plan to pique her interest seemed to be working. Perhaps over a slice of one of her grandmother's delicious pies, they could find some common ground and maybe he'd get a step or two closer to breaking down her wall.

Mary Penner was quite a challenge, which would have had his mother asking if that was her appeal. Abe remembered his mother's spunk. She never backed down from anyone, and she always had a quick quip. Dad had married the same type of woman Abe knew he wanted.

With a chuckle and a lighter step, Abe dressed in his Sunday finest trousers, a white shirt, and a vest he'd pulled out from the back of the closet. The one he wore last week had become frayed from age.

He stepped out on the front porch in time to see the cloud of dust billowing as his ride turned onto his property. David was right on time. As soon as the car stopped, Abe ambled over and got into the passenger seat. He snapped the seat belt in place.

"I appreciate you picking me up again, David. I know it's a lot to ask a man to work on Sunday."

"My pleasure. I'm starting to feel like we're old friends."

Abe adjusted his shirt and vest as David pulled onto the asphalt beyond the long driveway. His mother had made him this shirt years ago, but he hadn't worn it much because she wanted him to save it for something special.

David glanced at him then turned back to face the road. "You look nice, Abe. New duds?"

"Same kind of thing I always wear." Abe kept his focus straight ahead.

"Right." David snickered. "Will she be there?"

"If you're talking about Mary, yes, I imagine she will be. I don't think she or her grandparents ever miss church."

"My wife always goes to church, and sometimes I go with her to make her happy."

Abe turned to face David. "That seems strange to me. Why wouldn't you want to go all the time?"

David shrugged. "It's just not my thing."

"What if the Lord were to think the same of you?"

As they came to a stop sign, David nodded. "Good point. I never really thought about it like that."

"If you only do what is. . .your *thing*, then some of the important things might not get done." Abe paused, and when David didn't say anything, he continued. "God created us and gave us these lives, so why wouldn't we show our appreciation and worship Him as He instructed us to?"

David grinned. "Have you been talking to my wife? You sound just like her."

"Your wife is obviously a wise woman. Maybe you should listen to her more."

"I think I just might do that. In fact, I'm going to go straight home after I drop you off and tell her I'm going to church with her. She might fall over dead from shock."

"Or jump up and down with joy," Abe countered.

"That would be good. Thanks, buddy. I think you're good for me."

"The Lord puts people into our lives for a reason. You and I are good for each other."

"Yeah, we are." David stopped the van in front of the

church, where several families had already gathered. "What time do you want me to pick you up?"

"Mind if I call? I plan to stay for the potluck afterward, and that can go on for a while."

"That's fine. I'll make sure I turn my cell phone on after I get out of church so I don't miss your call. I'll be taking a few people home right after church, but I should be available."

Abe got out, closed the door, and waved to David before turning and walking toward the church. Ruthie, one of the girls from school who was still single, shyly lifted her hand in a greeting as he approached the front door.

"Hi, Ruthie. Nice day, eh?"

"Ya, it's a very nice day." Her sister standing behind her nudged her, causing her to lose her balance.

Abe reached out and gave her a steadying hand. "Whoa there, Ruthie."

Ruthie looked flustered as she glanced back at her sister, who stood there grinning. "Thank you, Abe. I—"

"Hi there, Abe!" a deep voice from behind bellowed.

Abe turned around to see Joseph Penner, followed by his wife, Sarah, and Mary trailing behind. He was sure Mary saw him, but she didn't look him in the eye.

"Excuse me, Ruthie, but I want to talk to someone."

"Ya, it was good seeing you, Abe."

As he walked away from Ruthie, he overheard her sister asking why she didn't say more. Ruthie was a nice girl, but she didn't have the ability to send his senses soaring the way Mary did.

Joseph stopped in front of Abe, and Sarah glanced over her shoulder, where Mary stood fidgeting with the folds of her skirt. Abe wanted to step past Mary's grandparents and talk to her, but he wasn't about to be rude.

"So how's the farm coming along?" Joseph asked.

"Bumper crop. Cows are all producing. Couldn't be better."

Abe's gaze locked with Mary's, and he saw a tiny twitch of amusement. His mouth suddenly went dry.

"That's good. The Glick farm has always been a good producer."

"Let me know what you need for the restaurant, and I'll make sure you have it."

"Thank you. You're a fine man, Abe."

Abe flashed a polite smile at Joseph before leaning around to look at Mary. "Will you be staying for the potluck, Mary?"

"Yes," she replied. "What else do you think I'd be doing?"

"Mary!" Sarah glared at her granddaughter before shaking her head as she looked at Abe. "I apologize for my granddaughter."

"Oh that's quite all right. I understand."

Mary narrowed her eyes as her lips puckered. It took every ounce of self-restraint for Abe not to laugh.

"We best be getting inside," Joseph said. "You and Mary can talk later."

Throughout the service, Abe cast occasional glances Mary's way. Once or twice he thought he might have caught her looking back at him, but she'd become a master of avoidance. He understood, based on her past and all, but he wished he could break through her shell enough for her to trust him. That was his first goal, and he knew it wouldn't be easy.

After the sermon, some children went up front and sang a cappella. The sweetness of their voices moved Abe. When he glanced at Mary, his heart melted at the sight of tears glistening in her eyes, obviously the result of her emotions tugging at her as his did him.

❧

Mary's heart ached at the memory of her own childhood and how much she missed out on. Instead of being here with other children, singing, she'd been darting about, running away from men with her mother. Sunday mornings had been the only time they'd spent together, but never in church. A few times Mama had tried to explain who God was, but her attempts were awkward. Until Mary came here to live with Grandma and Grandpa, all she'd thought about God was that He was cruel, and His only intent was to punish anyone who strayed from the very narrow path He'd laid before them.

Abe's lingering gaze did little to quell her sadness. He'd been just like those children, singing his heart out for the Lord while the adults listened with rapt attention. All this did was serve as another reminder of why she and Abe weren't meant to be together. No matter what Grandma and Grandpa said, Mary still didn't quite fit in. But she wasn't cut out for her former life either.

Mary still felt like an island—so alone and without anyone who could see how much she hurt inside. And she didn't dare let anyone know, in case her mother had been right. When she was younger, she thought that if anyone had any idea of all she'd seen, she'd be cast out of the community and never allowed back in. Now that she was older and realized she wasn't being shunned, all she felt was shame.

Grandma and Grandpa loved her. They knew her mother had done some bad things, and they even knew what some of those things were. But if they had any idea how much unmentionable decadence Mary had been exposed to, even they would have reason to pause before letting her into their home. She'd covered for her mother by lying to bosses and other men. They'd run away in the middle of the night a couple of times, and once when a man came looking for her mother asking for money he said she'd stolen, Mary had told him a string of lies to make him go away. Mary shuddered. She'd been an accessory to many evils that she never wanted anyone to know about. But the Lord knew, so she'd never be able to completely escape her shame.

Grandpa tried to show a soft side with her, but Grandma's sternness was real and there all the time. Mama had loved Mary, but she obviously didn't have the judgment or discernment she needed to take care of a child. As much as Mary loved Mama, she wished she'd started out with the safety and shelter she now knew.

Abe caught her attention and smiled. She tried to smile back, but her chin quivered, and she had to look away.

Mary was relieved when the children finished the last of their songs. Music stirred her spirit to the point of dredging up even more of her past than she wanted to remember. After the singing was over and the pastor ended the service, everyone filed outside where the men had set up the tables and Grandma and a few of the other women had begun arranging the food. Mary tried to stay invisible as she helped.

Before she even heard his voice, Mary felt Abe's presence behind her. "That was a very touching service," he said softly. She turned to face him, and he lowered his head so only she could hear him. "I saw that you felt it, too. How sweet the sound of young, innocent voices."

Mary managed a small smile, and she nodded. "Yes, they were very sweet."

"I vaguely remember standing there singing for the congregation when I was a boy. If I knew then what I know now. . ." Abe chuckled. "Famous last words of many a man."

"Abe!"

They turned to see Grandpa heading toward them. "Don't look now, but I think we're about to have a chaperone."

"Mary, your grandmother needs you over by the dessert table." He looked at Abe. "You don't mind, do you?"

"For the sake of my sweet tooth, by all means, please see what your grandmother needs." Abe gestured toward the food. "I don't think anyone will leave hungry."

"I'll go see what she wants," Mary said as she took off toward the cluster of women arranging pies, cakes, and cookies. Deep down she was glad to have something else to do. All that talk about the innocence of children conjured up memories that had kept her up many nights.

Mary passed one table laden with various versions of potato salad, coleslaw, and an assortment of other cold vegetable dishes. The table on the other side hosted platters of roast beef, ham, and chicken. Abe was right. No one would go hungry today.

She'd barely arrived by her grandmother's side when the older woman shoved a platter of cookies toward her. "Take this to that extra table we're setting up." Grandma pointed to a bare table about twenty feet away. "We got more desserts than we expected."

Mary busied herself with mindless tasks, helping get everything organized. As people filled their plates with what had been laid out earlier, quite a few more dishes seemed to appear by the minute.

After the women were finished, the pastor asked everyone to gather so he could bless the meal. Everyone held hands. One of the children who'd sung earlier stood on one side of Mary, and Grandma's friend Helga was on the other. After the blessing, the little girl let go and scampered off, but Helga squeezed Mary's hand and pulled her in for a hug.

"You are a good girl, Mary."

"Thank you." Mary leaned away, but Helga still didn't let go.

"You do realize your grandparents love you very much, don't you?"

"Yes, of course."

"Your grandmother still struggles with Elizabeth's departure. Please understand how difficult that was for her."

Mary nodded as she wondered what Grandma had told Helga. She didn't know what to say, so she remained quiet.

"Sometimes I think Sarah is a little bit too stern with you, but I think she's afraid to loosen up for fear of something bad happening."

"I understand," Mary said softly.

"Do you really?" Helga released her grip and placed one hand on Mary's shoulder. "I know it can't be easy when you feel like someone is always angry. My mother was like that, after my sister left and never came back."

"I—I'm sorry. I didn't know about that."

Helga dropped her hand from Mary's shoulder and tilted her head. "Some people don't understand how blessed they are, and they go looking for happiness outside what brings true joy."

"Yes, I know."

"You'll be just fine, sweetheart. Now what's this I hear about Abe courting you?"

"Oh, we're just friends."

Helga leaned back and laughed. "Sure you are. Mary, you need to open your eyes and see how that man looks at you. He's smitten, even if you're not."

Once again Helga had rendered Mary speechless. She smiled and shrugged.

"Looks like the rest of the men are all in line now, so let's join the others, shall we?" Helga didn't wait for an answer before taking Mary by the hand and leading her over to the crowd around the tables.

After Mary filled her plate, she glanced around until she spotted Abe sitting at a table with some of the children. There was an empty place next to him. She wondered if he might be saving it for her. She was about to walk toward him when Ruthie plopped her plate on the table, and she sat down next to Abe. A stabbing sensation shot through Mary's chest, and she forced herself to turn away.

"Over here, Mary," Helga said, her hand lifted in the air. "We saved you a spot."

Thankful for a place to go, Mary darted over to where Helga, Helga's husband, Paul, her grandparents, and a few other people their age sat. As she passed some of the people she knew from school, some of them looked away as though pretending they didn't see her. Before sitting down, she looked around for Shelley.

"Who are you looking for?" Helga asked.

"Shelley. Do you know if she's here?"

"Her brother is sick, so she left right after church to help his wife," Grandma replied without looking up.

Mary suspected the reason Shelley was so kind to her was that her older brother had left the church before Mary met her, so she knew some things were out of Mary's control. Shelley still didn't understand all Mary had experienced.

"These rolls are excellent, Sarah," one of the other ladies at the table said to Grandma. "What's your secret?"

"Butter," Grandma replied. "Lots of it."

"Butter makes everything better."

"Looks like the tourists are coming early."

"Ya," Paul said. "And they like their ice cream."

Everyone smiled and nodded. "Your ice cream is the best there is."

"So I've been told." A few people laughed.

"You better make some pies and freeze them, Sarah. With all these tourists coming to Sarasota, they'll be wanting dessert every day."

"I might have to teach my granddaughter how to make pies instead of having her wait on tables, taking orders."

Mary nodded. "I'll do whatever you need."

Helga nudged her. "I don't know if it's such a good idea to stick Mary back in the kitchen. She's still a young girl. She needs to be around people."

Grandma snorted. "She's around people in church. I don't think she needs to be around all the customers."

Mary squirmed. She hated people talking about her. Helga reached for her hand and offered a conspiratorial smile before turning to face the others. "I hope this weather stays nice for a while."

That was all it took for the conversation to turn to weather. "It's gonna be a hot summer," one of the men said.

Helga leaned toward her and whispered, "Abe keeps looking over here. I bet he wishes you were there instead of Ruthie."

"I'm sure he's just fine sitting next to her." Mary used every ounce of self-restraint to keep from glancing in Abe's direction.

❧

Abe strained to see around some people who stood between him and Mary.

"I haven't been to your family farm since you added the barn," Ruthie said. "I hear it's huge."

"Ya." Abe stuffed another bite of roll into his mouth, chewed it, and glanced over toward Mary. "It's big, but I have a lot of cows. I need a big barn."

"A dairy farm is a good business, according to my father. He says a man who has land and animals will never have to depend on anyone else to survive."

"I s'pose your father is right."

Ruthie put down her fork, placed her hands in her lap, leaned back, and sighed. "It's such a beautiful day. Perfect for a long walk, don't you think, Abe?"

"Ya, it is indeed a very nice day." He knew what Ruthie was hinting at, but he didn't want to go for a walk with her. He wanted to be with Mary, who wouldn't even turn around and look at him.

"Would you. . .um. . ." Ruthie swallowed and fidgeted.

Abe took advantage of her nervousness and stood. "Thank you for your company, Ruthie, but I have to talk to some people. See you around, okay?" He smiled as warmly as he could.

She looked dejected, but she quickly recovered. "Ya. See you around. Will you be in church next week?"

"You know I'm always in church on Sunday."

"Ya, that is true."

"Bye, Ruthie." Abe felt terrible. He hated hurting people's feelings, but he couldn't justify sitting there letting Ruthie think something might happen between them when he really wanted to be with Mary instead.

He suspected Ruthie was watching him as he made his way over to where Mary sat with her grandparents and all their friends. One by one, they looked up at him as he arrived.

"Hi, Abe. Did you enjoy the potluck?" Helga asked as she leaned back to give him a clear view of Mary.

When his gaze met Helga's, he saw the depth of her understanding. A smile crept across her face, and her eyes twinkled as she grinned. He couldn't help but smile back.

"Yes, it was delicious." He turned to Mary. "Would you like to take a walk with me, Mary?"

"Um. . ." She looked at her grandpa, who gave a crisp nod. "That sounds good." Then she paused for a moment. "But I have to help the women clean up."

"Here," Helga said, handing her some plates. "Take these to the sink in the church kitchen and consider your part of the cleanup done."

"I'll help," Abe offered.

Before anyone said a word, he walked around the table and gathered some plates. Several of the men got up and started helping out as well. This started a snowball effect as everyone pitched in. In less than fifteen minutes, most of the yard had been cleared away.

"C'mon, Mary, let's go." Abe placed his hand on her shoulder and led her away from the crowd.

five

The streets were beginning to fill with cars, with license plates from a variety of northern states and Canada. The first of the summer tourists had made their mark on the town. Occasionally one of the members of the local Mennonite or Amish community passed them on a three-wheeler. Mary didn't have much experience in Mennonite communities outside the one in Sarasota, but she'd heard about the horse and buggies in Ohio and Pennsylvania, where many of her grandparents' friends were from. Some of them came from communities where they rarely had contact with Yankees. Here in Sarasota, that was impossible.

Once they were a block away, Abe looked down at Mary and grinned. The softness in his gaze turned her insides to mush.

"What's wrong, Mary?" He slowed down his pace a bit.

"Nothing's wrong. It's just that. . ." How could she explain that whenever he gave her that look, she felt the world was spinning, but she enjoyed the ride? How could she tell him how much she loved being with him, but she didn't know what to think or how to act? Abe got her senses all out of sync. And then there was the issue of not knowing what he wanted. And all men wanted something, didn't they?

"You can talk to me, Mary. I want to get to know you better."

"We've known each other nine—"

"I know." Abe snorted. "You keep reminding me. We've known each other a long time, but how well do we really *know* each other?"

"Well, I know you have a big farm." Mary held up one finger then lifted another. "And you like to eat at my grandparents' restaurant." She raised a third finger. "You love bread and lots of grease."

"Not that kind of stuff, Mary. I'm talking about knowing someone deep down." He made a fist and touched his chest. "Things that really matter."

"I don't know. There are some things we probably shouldn't know about each other."

"Like what?" he asked.

"Why would I tell you anything?"

"Because I care?" Abe stopped, gripped her shoulder, and turned her around to face him. "Because I've liked you since I first met you."

"So you've said." She couldn't help her eyes widening as he continued to watch her, almost as though waiting for something. "But why?"

"I wish I knew. It's strange. When you walked into the classroom years ago, I saw something in your eyes that grabbed my heart."

Mary had to stifle a gasp. "I don't understand what you're saying, Abe."

"Okay, let me spell it out for you. I like you a lot, Mary Penner, and I want to spend time with you and see if you're the woman God wants for me." He held her gaze, making her insides flutter again. "I think you and I are meant to be together."

"I don't think you know what you're saying."

"Oh, but I do. Do you not like me?"

"I like you just fine, Abe."

"Then what's the problem? I like you, you like me. We can share our thoughts and feelings, and maybe. . ."

"What if you find out some stuff about me that makes you not like me anymore?" she asked.

"Or what if you find out something you don't like about me?" He tilted his head and snickered. "That could happen, you know." He took her hand and led her to a more secluded spot, away from the street.

Her heart thudded. "I'm sure it could."

"Mary Penner, I have a question for you."

She tensed. Questions generally led her someplace she didn't want to go. "What is it?"

"Do you mind if I kiss you?"

Mary slowly turned her face up toward his again. As he lowered his lips to hers, an odd sensation ripped at her stomach. She pulled away. "No, don't."

A wisp of hair escaped her kapp and fell across her forehead, then covered one of her eyes. Abe lifted it and gently tucked it behind her ear.

"You're beautiful, Mary."

No one had ever told her she was beautiful. She was momentarily paralyzed and speechless. Abe continued staring down at her face, his gaze traveling from her eyes to her mouth then back to her eyes.

A shiver washed over her as her mother's words popped into her mind. *Never believe a man who flatters you, Mary. It just means he wants something.* She shuddered.

Abe tilted his head. "Are you cold?"

She shook her head. "No, but I need to get back."

"What just happened, Mary?"

"Nothing." How could she explain the turmoil inside her—the sensation of wanting to be with Abe but not trusting his intentions? As much as she wanted him to kiss her and hold her close, her mother's voice continued to play in her head.

He stood staring at the ground for a few seconds before he offered a hand. "C'mon, I'll walk you home."

"I think I'd rather walk home by myself."

"But—" Abe stopped himself then frowned. "Okay, but I don't understand. You are a very confusing woman."

"I'm sorry." She turned away from him and started half-walking, half-running toward her grandparents' house with a heavy heart.

"I don't give up easily," he called out. "You'll see me again soon, Mary Penner."

She broke into a full run until she was nearly a block away. Then she stopped, sucked in a breath, and looked around at the tiny houses that surrounded her. Pinecraft was home now, but she felt isolated, even in familiar territory. Memories of her childhood continued to flood her mind. The first thing she remembered was when she was very small—maybe three or four years old. Her mother had just handed her over to a woman who took in children while their parents worked the night shift.

"I'll be back in the morning," Mama had said in her usual weary tone. Mary watched her mother walk away, shoulders sagging as the weight of her life dragged her down. Even now, nearly twenty years later, she remembered feeling an overwhelming sadness and despondency.

As Mary slowly trudged home to her grandparents' house, more images and scenes popped into her head. Through the years, Mama had a variety of jobs, but she'd discovered the highest paying ones were in bars, which had turned out to be a disaster for both of them.

When Mary turned twelve, Mama announced that she trusted Mary to stay home alone. "Just stay inside and don't answer the door. You'll be asleep while I'm gone, so everything should be okay."

But everything wasn't okay. Mary always had a tough time falling asleep in the tiny one-bedroom apartment they'd managed to keep for almost a year. They'd been booted out of all their other homes because her mother couldn't afford the rent when it came due.

Vivid scenes of men coming and going made Mary sick to her stomach. She suspected she missed quite a bit while she was in school, and she was thankful for it. As it was, she saw more than a child should see in a lifetime. But the one scene that she'd dreaded remembering came crashing through her mind, and she couldn't stop it. It was the night when her life completely changed.

Mama had left for work a little after nine and told her to go on to bed—said that she'd be back when Mary got up. As always, Mary lay in bed with the covers pulled to her chin, shivering from fear of darkness, waiting for sleep to come. . . to overtake her and pull her from the conscious nightmare she'd suffered ever since Mama had taken that job at the bar down the street. Mary didn't know what Mama did, and she didn't want to know.

She'd started to feel the wooziness that preceded drifting off to sleep when she heard the loud banging on the door. At first she didn't want to answer it, but a low voice from the hallway let out the code word she and Mama had established. So she wrapped the blanket around her shoulders and made her way to the door. She left the chain latched as she opened the door a few inches. The man handed her an envelope through the tiny opening, then took off running.

After he was out of sight, she closed the door and fastened the dead bolt then turned on the light in the living room. The outside of the envelope had the words *In case of emergency, deliver to my daughter, Mary* scrawled across the front. Mary ripped it open and pulled out the pink-lined paper. The note was in her mother's handwriting. With shaky fingers, she read that she was to call Big Jim at the phone number beneath his name.

The details of that night remained a blur. All she remembered was calling Big Jim and learning her mother had been killed. It had something to do with a drug bust and her mama being an informant. She didn't believe him, so she dropped the phone and ran to the bar to find her mother. Instead she found Big Jim in his office that reeked of cigar smoke and stale beer. Big Jim gave Mary some money, bought her a bus ticket, and told her he'd sent word to Elizabeth's parents letting them know their fourteen-year-old granddaughter was on her way. He added that he'd tried to warn her mother that she was in dangerous territory by agreeing to help the police, but she thought the money the police promised her would help make a better life for her and Mary.

"Go home and get your things. I'll pick you up and take you to the bus station," Big Jim said before pausing and turning. "Oh, I almost forgot. I have something your mother wanted me to give you." Big Jim's son, Jimbo, sat on the floor in the corner of his dad's small office, glaring at Mary with beady eyes and a scowl. She shivered at the memory.

Big Jim had handed her a small box and instructed her not to open it until she was safely with her grandparents. He even made her promise. As she nodded her promise, she couldn't help but notice the smirk that had formed on Jimbo's face. She shuddered at some of the memories she had of that horrible boy.

To this day, she still hadn't opened the box. She'd lived this long not knowing what it was. Why would she want to do anything that would bring back such horrible memories? But they were still in her head. And that tiny box lay on the floor in the corner of her closet, serving as a reminder that she had a past no one in Pinecraft would ever understand.

❧

Frustrated and perplexed, Abe stood on the street, waiting for his ride. David had sounded surprised to hear from him so soon.

"I just dropped off the last family, so your timing was good."

Abe opened his mouth to say something but quickly closed it. Then he sighed.

"I don't have to ask what happened," David said as soon as Abe got into the car. "It's written all over your face." He shook his head. "Women."

"Something happened to her," Abe said. "She seemed fine to a point, but when I asked her. . ." He looked down at his hands steepled in his lap. "I asked her if I could kiss her, and she just. . .well, she acted frightened."

"That's where you went wrong, buddy. If you wanna kiss a girl, you don't ask, you just do it. That way she can't turn you down."

"Mary is different."

"Maybe so, but it looks to me like she wouldn't mind if you kissed her, as long as it happens by surprise."

Abe stared at David. "What makes you say that?"

David cast a quick smile in Abe's direction. "I've seen how she looks at you. She likes you, Abe. In fact, she likes you very much."

If Abe could be sure David was right, he'd be willing to take his advice. But David obviously didn't know how bad Mary's past experiences might have been, and he certainly didn't want to be the one to tell him.

"Give it a shot, Abe. You like her, she likes you. What have you got to lose? She's Mennonite. She won't slap you, right?"

David had a point. "Ya, I don't think she'll slap me."

"Now that we've got that settled, my wife wanted to know if you planned to have some of your delicious vegetables at the produce market on Saturday."

"Ya, I always do. I'm not sure yet who will be working it."

"If you're in the same place, I'll just tell her to go there. She said your citrus was better than anyone else's." David turned at the farm entrance. "I'd like my wife to meet you one of these days."

"Why?"

David grinned. "She's fascinated by the things I tell her about you."

"I don't know what would be so fascinating about me. My life is very plain and simple."

"Plain, maybe," David agreed before lifting an eyebrow. "But not simple." He came to a stop and repeated, "Definitely not simple. You seem to have pretty much the same issues people who aren't Mennonite have, only you have a different way of dealing with them."

Abe opened the car door but paused before getting out. "Matters of the heart are never simple, are they?"

"You got that right." David waved as Abe got out of the car.

ॐ

"I'm not hungry, Grandma," Mary said. "I think I'll pass on supper tonight."

Grandma gave her a sideways glance. "I don't want you tossing and turning all night because your stomach starts rumbling."

Mary patted her stomach. "I don't think that'll happen. I ate enough at the church to last the rest of the day."

Instead of responding, Grandma turned back to preparing the food. Mary left the kitchen and went outside. As she stood in the front yard, she glanced around at the children playing in the yard a few houses down. Occasionally she thought about having her own family, and there were even times she longed for a husband and children. The women in the neighborhood seemed content in their marriages.

Mama's words about men always wanting something rang through her mind constantly, but sometimes Mary wondered how true they were. It was obvious that Mama's experiences had been different from these women's. However, Mary also remembered what Mama had told her about being shunned by her own community, and there was never any doubt her mother had told her the truth—at least from her perspective. They hadn't exactly been warm and welcoming to Mary in the beginning. A few people, like Shelley. . .and Abe. . . treated her well, but many of the others acted as though she had some disease they might catch if they so much as had a conversation with her. No one had been openly mean, but even now people seemed afraid to hold a conversation with her. She thought about what Abe had said—that her shame made her standoffish, which in turn kept people away.

She stood in the front yard and watched a couple of neighborhood children playing ball. The older boy was kind and considerate of the younger one's lack of coordination. Seeing these boys playing made her think about all she'd missed as a child. She wondered if she'd ever be a mother, and if so, how she'd handle questions about her past.

Mary watched the boys until their mother called them inside. Then she headed back into her grandparents' house. Grandma and Grandpa were in the kitchen reading their Bibles. The aroma of Grandma's homemade vegetable soup still hung in the air.

"Join us, Mary," Grandpa said, patting her place at the table. "We were just reading from the book of Luke."

"Luke 21:34," Grandma added. "You may read next if you like."

Mary nodded as she pulled her Bible from the small shelf Grandpa had built next to the table. She flipped through the pages and began to read.

"Be careful or your hearts will be weighed down with carousing, drunkenness and the anxieties of life. . ."

As the words flowed from Mary's lips, she could feel the intensity of how relevant they were to her life. She'd seen the results of what happened when people got caught up in sins of the flesh. What a bitter existence. The life she had now was one of simplicity and very little focus on worrying about things. At times like this, the peace that washed through her soul reminded her of how blessed she was.

She finished the verse and glanced up in time to see Grandma wipe a tear from her cheek. Grandpa's foot lightly touched Mary's beneath the table. As their gazes met, she saw how concerned he was for Grandma.

Mary started to get up, but Grandpa motioned for her to sit back down. "Your grandmother and I have been talking. . . ." He glanced over at his wife, who nodded for him to continue. "What happened to us the day you arrived was both tragic and joyful. We lost one daughter—for the second time—and gained a granddaughter we always longed to see. But the most tragic thing that happened was losing our daughter the first time—back when she found something she preferred over what we offered her."

"I–I'm sorry," Mary said.

"You shouldn't be sorry," Grandpa said with a forced smile beneath glistening, moist eyes. "You are the joy that came out of the sadness. We love you very much, and we want you to be as content as we are. The Lord has blessed us greatly."

Mary turned to Grandma for a check on her reaction, and she was surprised to see her also smiling. "Ya, we love you very much, Mary. I know I don't always show how much—"

"She knows you love her, Sarah." Grandpa looked at Mary with his head tilted toward her. "We're concerned about you, though. There is no joy in your life. All you do is go to the restaurant and then come home. We were hoping you and Abe. . .well, that maybe you two would hit it off."

"Abe is a fine man," Grandma added. "He will take care of you, and you will always know you're safe."

Mary looked down at her hands clasped tightly in her lap. She wasn't sure if she'd ever feel safe—no matter where she was or who she was with. Even here with Grandma and Grandpa, in her mind the safest place on earth, there were times she wasn't sure she was wanted.

Grandpa shifted in his seat, capturing Mary's attention. "I know you have some painful memories, Granddaughter, and there's nothing we can do about that except pray. But it's time you learned to trust other people."

Mary nodded. "I trust both of you."

"Ya," he said, "but you need to trust that the Lord has put Abe into your life for a reason." He paused before adding, "And you need to trust Abe with your heart."

Mary knew Grandpa meant well, but it was easier for him to say than for her to take his advice. "I'd like to," she whispered.

"Let's pray about this," Grandpa said as he pulled one of her hands from the other. He reached for Grandma's hand, and they all bowed their heads.

After the prayer, Grandpa released her hand. Mary kept her eyes squeezed shut and silently added her own thoughts and feelings. *Lord, I want to be the woman You want me to be. Please show me the way, and I'll try. . .no, I'll make it my plan to do Your will.*

When she opened her eyes, both of her grandparents had gotten up. Grandpa had left the room, but Grandma was over by the sink with her back turned toward Mary.

"I'm washing the pot I left to soak after supper," Grandma said.

"Need help?"

"No, I'm almost done." Grandma dumped the water from the pot and dried it with the dish towel before putting it back in the cupboard. "I heard you talking to that little boy. Maybe someday you'll have children of your own."

"Maybe."

Grandma sighed. "I would have had a houseful if I could.

Your mama was such a cheerful little girl, I thought a dozen more just like her would be perfect." She sniffled and wiped her cheek with her sleeve. "The Lord obviously didn't feel I should have more children. When we lost Elizabeth, your grandpa and I felt like our breath had been taken away. Worldly living does that to so many people. I didn't want her to go up to Cincinnati to stay with those girls. I was afraid she'd never come back. When she did, I was so happy, I sang all the time. Then. . ." She hung her head. "As each day passed, the light in your mama's eyes faded a little bit more. I knew something was wrong, but until I realized what she'd done and that she was pregnant, I couldn't figure it out."

Mary wanted to hear more about the specifics of what happened on the day Mama left from Grandma's perspective, but she didn't want to push for answers. She didn't want to create tension.

"Mama missed you and Grandpa," Mary said, her voice catching on emotion.

"Did she tell you that?" The expectant look on Grandma's face tempted Mary to lie, but she couldn't.

She shook her head. "No, she never actually came right out and said that, but I could tell. She was lonely." And she cried when she didn't think Mary could hear her.

"So was I. Some days, every time I heard a sound outside, I ran to the door, hoping it was my Elizabeth."

Mary wanted to ask more questions—like what would have happened if she and her mother had shown up. But it seemed that questions caused Grandma to clam up. She was much more open when she spoke of her own volition.

Grandma folded the towel and hung it from the drawer handle, then turned and looked Mary squarely in the eye. "I used to worry that when you turned sixteen, you would do what your Mama did."

Mary slowly shook her head. "No, I would never have done

that. It wasn't a good life."

They held gazes for almost a minute before Grandma closed the gap between them and wrapped her arms around Mary. At first Mary was so stunned she froze. Then she slowly relaxed, melting into Grandma's embrace and allowing the older woman's warmth to provide the comfort she needed. They held on to each other until Grandma finally let go and gently held Mary at arm's length.

"You are a delightful young woman, with a lot to offer the right man."

Mary gulped. "I want to do what God calls me to do." She dropped her gaze to the floor.

"Yes, I know that now." Grandma lifted Mary's chin and looked her in the eye. "Do you ever think what it would be like to find a husband and have your own home?"

six

Mary lay in bed staring at the ceiling with the light from outside casting a faint glow through the thin curtains. Usually before she fell asleep, she reflected on the day and how far she'd come from her past. Tonight was different. She'd had some sort of emotional connection to Grandma that she never thought possible. Grandma's question about whether or not she wanted a husband and home of her own played through her mind, and Abe's image instantly appeared.

She squeezed her eyes shut and asked the Lord to give her the wisdom she needed. Abe had already made his intentions clear, and Grandma seemed to think she should try to have a normal Mennonite life.

Mary wanted a normal life, but it never seemed possible for her to have one. Her rough early years haunted her everywhere she went. When she'd first moved to Sarasota, she doubted everyone's motives for talking to her, including Grandma and Grandpa's. It hadn't taken long to learn to trust Grandpa. Even though Mama had said men always wanted something, Mary sensed a strong relationship between Mama and Grandpa that her mother missed, or at least hadn't told her about. Mama had complained about Grandpa being cold, but Mary didn't see that in him. Grandma was a different story. According to Mama, Grandma was a vindictive old woman who didn't understand what it was like to be young. At first, after coming to live with her grandparents, Mary agreed with Mama, but through the years, she occasionally saw a softening that escaped

Grandma's stern facade for a few minutes or seconds. Until recently.

Now everything was different. After Grandma's talk with her during their walk, her demeanor had gradually softened even more. Mary's thoughts swirled around all the conversations she'd had with Abe and how her grandparents were encouraging her to be with him. As her swirling thoughts gradually slowed, Mary finally relaxed and allowed sleep to wash over her.

She awakened the next morning with the determination to explore her relationship with Abe. Her feelings couldn't be denied, and she needed to put a stop to the negative thoughts that crept into her head. Mama's words had been spoken during the worst of all times. Mary was now much older than Mama had been when she'd left the safety and security of her family's home. Their lives were totally different.

Grandma stood at the stove stirring something in a small pot. Without turning around, she asked, "Want some oatmeal before you go in to work this morning, or would you rather eat there?"

Mary pulled a bowl from the cupboard and set it down next to the stove. "I'll eat before I go in." She leaned against the counter. "I've been thinking about our conversation last night."

Grandma sighed. "Sometimes you think too much. If you keep doing that, you'll talk yourself out of happiness."

Mary laughed. "Not this time. I've decided to get to know Abe better and see how things go with him."

"You've known that boy for nine years, child. How much longer do you need to know him?"

Abe's words from when she'd cast out the same argument flittered through her head. "I want to know more about him as a man. If I went on the way he acted when we were kids, I'd run fast in the other direction."

Grandma cast a dubious look at Mary, then went back to

stirring. "He couldn't have been that bad."

"He wasn't, but at the time I didn't like it. His teasing irritated me."

"Hand me your bowl." Grandma took the bowl from Mary's hands and scooped some oatmeal into it. "So what do you plan to do to get to know Abe better?"

"I'll start by accepting when he asks me to do things."

"I thought you already did that."

"I did, but I didn't make it easy for him. I've been very defensive around Abe. That will change now."

"Good. Now eat your oatmeal and get out of here so you can help with the breakfast crowd. I'll be in after I get the kitchen cleaned up."

Mary gulped down her oatmeal then rinsed her bowl. She got her tote from her room, went outside, and put the bag in the basket of her three-wheeler.

She'd always enjoyed the ride to work in semidarkness, when Sarasota still seemed like a sleepy little town. In just a couple of hours, they'd have bumper-to-bumper traffic and the sounds that went with it.

From the moment she walked into the restaurant, Mary was busy waiting on tables, busing tables, and helping out in the kitchen. Her focus was on giving her customers—mostly tourists—what they needed.

"Mary."

The soft male voice behind Mary stopped her. She slowly pivoted until she was looking into Abe Glick's warm brown eyes. Her lips twitched as she smiled at him.

His eyebrows shot up as surprise registered on his face. "You must be having a good morning."

"Yes." Mary nodded as she held his gaze. "A very good morning."

Abe nodded toward a booth in the back. "Mind if I seat myself over there?"

"That would be just fine. I'll bring you a menu. Want coffee?"

"Don't worry about the menu. I know what I want. Just bring coffee, and I'll give you my order."

"Okay, I'll have it to you in two shakes of a horse's tail."

Abe leaned away and grinned. "You certainly are in a good mood this morning. I don't know if I've ever seen you like this before."

Suddenly it struck Mary. Maybe Abe wouldn't like her if he didn't feel like he had to cheer her up. "Is that a bad thing?"

"Neh. I like it."

"Well, good. Go have a seat, and I'll be right there."

Mary didn't waste any time getting Abe his coffee. She laid the napkin-wrapped fork, knife, and spoon on the table in front of him before lifting her order pad.

"So how would you like your sugar and grease this morning, Mr. Glick?"

The corners of his eyes crinkled as he chuckled. "What would you think if I told you I'll eat whatever you think I should have?"

"Doesn't matter what I think. The question is, will you really eat it?"

Abe leaned back and studied her. "I think so. Just make sure there's an egg or two on my plate, and I'll eat pretty much anything."

She jotted that down and gave him a clipped nod. "Coming right up. Mystery breakfast with an egg or two."

※

Abe had entered Penner's with the intention of observing Mary then going home for the rest of the day. However, the way she was acting led him to believe things had changed. He thought she might be open to doing something with him later.

He sipped his coffee and watched Mary wait on other customers while the folks in the kitchen prepared his breakfast. He didn't have to wait long before she brought him a plate laden with fresh fruit, one of her grandmother's famous bran muffins, and two poached eggs.

"No gruel?" he asked playfully.

"Nope. It's all good for you, and it tastes good, too." She took a step back and smiled over her shoulder. "Anything else I can do for you, Abe?"

"Ya."

Mary stopped and turned completely toward him. "Okay, now what?"

"You can go with me to have some ice cream later. I know you have to work, but maybe after lunch?"

"Um. . ." She placed her index finger on her chin as a smile spread across her lips. "Sounds very good. I'd love to go have ice cream with you."

He tried not to show the shock over her lack of resistance. "I have to go home to do a few things on the farm, but I will be back. What time can you go?"

Mary glanced around at the crowd. "We're busy today, but I think things will slow down around three. I'll check with Grandpa before you finish your breakfast and make sure it's okay with him, but I think he'll be fine with that."

Abe picked up a muffin and held it up to her. "Sounds good."

He watched Mary scurry around the restaurant as he ate his breakfast. It wasn't as filling as what he was used to, but he thought it was sweet that Mary was conscious of his diet. Most people couldn't eat as much grease and sugar without increasing the size of their girth, but Abe was so busy on the farm, he worked it off. He'd be hungry again in a couple of hours, but he'd ask David to stop somewhere so he could grab a slice of ham and biscuit on the way back to the farm.

Before he was finished, he called David and asked if he could pick him up in ten minutes. David said that would be fine since he had some other people to pick up and drop off not far from the Glick farm.

After Abe paid, Joseph Penner approached him and put his hand on Abe's shoulder. "I'm happy to hear that you'll be back to see Mary later. I told her she could leave at two thirty if that's better."

"Neh, three o'clock is fine. I have to do some things on the farm, and that gives me just enough time to get back to town."

"I'll tell Mary," Mr. Penner said.

Abe saw David pull into the restaurant parking lot. "I gotta go. My ride is here. I look forward to seeing Mary this afternoon."

A couple of people were in the back of the van, but they were engrossed in conversation. Abe hopped into the front passenger seat.

As soon as Abe clicked his seat belt, the questions started. "Well? What did she say?"

"I'm coming back this afternoon and taking her out for ice cream."

"Good job, man. It won't be long before you're announcing your engagement."

"That would be good, but one thing I know about Mary is that she can't be rushed. I have to let her get used to the fact that she and I are meant to be together."

David snickered. "You're pretty sure about that, aren't you?"

"Never been more sure of anything in my life." Abe paused and faced David. "How about when you met your wife? Weren't you sure?"

"I knew I loved her, but the thought of it being a forever kind of relationship sort of scared me."

"What's to be scared of?" Abe asked. "Marriage is a sacred commitment between a man and woman."

David cleared his throat. "I think that's what scared me the most—that sacred commitment thing."

Abe shook his head. "Commitment is a good thing. It keeps us focused on the Lord's will."

"I wish I could be more like you, Abe. Your life is so simple and easy to figure out. I bet you don't have any debt, do you?"

"Neh, I only buy what I can afford. Why? Are you in debt?"

"Oh yeah. To the max."

"But why?"

David shrugged. "I dunno. It just sort of started with us wanting a car we couldn't afford, then it progressed to other things."

"You can do something about that if you want to."

"We're working on it. It took some doing, but I finally got my wife on board with the concept of following the biblical financial plan they offer at our church." He turned onto the shell road and pulled to a stop in front of Abe's house. "After she dragged me to church, I found the one thing that interested me was the financial program they offered."

Abe got out, reached deep into his pocket, and handed David a few extra dollars. "Add this to your fund, David. Get out of debt as soon as you possibly can, and you'll be much happier."

"You don't have to do that," David said as he looked at the wad of bills in his hand.

"I know I don't, but I want to."

"You're a good man, Abe—a very good man who will make some woman a wonderful husband. I hope things work out between you and Mary."

"I have to trust in the Lord's will. If Mary and I are meant to be together, it will happen. See you this afternoon around two thirty?"

David nodded. "I'll be here."

Abe closed the door, turned, and walked toward the house. He heard David's van heading back toward the highway.

As Abe walked up the path to his front door, one of his workers ran up to him with a question. The rest of the morning and early afternoon seemed to fly by, which suited Abe just fine. It kept his mind off Mary.

David arrived at two thirty, only this time he was in his car. "Where's the van?" Abe asked as he buckled his seat belt.

"The wife has been after me to hire someone to help me branch out and increase business, so I finally did. He has the van." David looked over his shoulder as he backed up to turn the car around. "I've found that my wife is generally right, but when you meet her, don't go telling her I said that."

Abe laughed. "It might be a good idea for you to tell her that."

"What? And let her think she can win all the arguments? Where's the fun in that?"

"I don't know about you, but I don't like to argue. I find it very upsetting. When I get married and my wife tells me something that helps, I will tell her."

"I'm sure you will." David focused his attention on the road until he was about a mile from Penner's. "Wanna call me when it's time to pick you up?"

"Neh, I'll be ready around four thirty."

"See you then," David said as he pulled to a stop in front of the restaurant. "If anything changes, you know how to get ahold of me."

Abe waved to David then turned around and found himself about three feet from Mary, who had an amused look on her face. "Good to see you again, Abe. Now let's go get some ice cream." Without another word, she reached for his arm and tucked her hand in the crook of his elbow.

୬

It took all of Mary's self-restraint not to laugh at Abe's

reaction. His eyes widened, and his chin dropped. "So how's the farm? Anything new?" she asked.

"Ya. Just this morning one of my workers told me about a new bull that's for sale. I told him to look him over and buy him if he thinks it's a good deal."

"A new bull, huh? How about that?"

"We just cleared the land for some more grapefruit trees, too."

Mary smiled. Abe's dedication to his farm was admirable.

The blaring sound of a honking horn snagged their attention. Mary scrunched her eyebrows. "Is that Jeremiah again?"

"Afraid so." Abe shook his head. "Ever since he left the church, he's been sort of wild."

"Sort of?" Mary snorted. "He came into the restaurant with some of his friends earlier. Grandpa had to ask them to quiet down or leave."

"He used to be such a good guy, but I do remember him talking about outsiders and how much fun they seemed to be having."

Jeremiah pulled to a stop beside them. "Hey, Abe. Wanna go for a ride in my new wheels?"

"Neh." Abe glanced down at Mary. "I'm on a date."

Mary started to grin, but Jeremiah's hoot cracked her joy. "Can't say I blame you. She's hot."

"Don't talk about her like that, Jeremiah." Mary saw Abe's jaw tighten. "She's a nice girl who deserves respect."

"Did you ever ask her about what she did before she joined the plain clothes brigade?" He cackled. "I bet she saw some action that would make you a very happy man."

Abe started to advance toward Jeremiah, but Mary held him back and walked up to Jeremiah alone. "You're a terrible man, Jeremiah. Just because you turned your back on God doesn't give you the right to try to pull someone as nice as Abe away."

"Wait, Mary, I can handle this," Abe said as he gently took her hand then stepped between her and the car. "Jeremiah, you better move along. You know I can't fight you, but I can contact the authorities."

Mary held her breath as she watched Jeremiah's expression go from jeering to acceptance. Finally he nodded. "I'll talk to you about it later, Abe. I don't want you missing out on a golden opportunity, now that you've got yourself a live one." He sped away, hooting and hollering and saying disrespectful things.

"I'm so sorry, Mary. You should never have to hear such words."

She flicked her hand. "It's nothing I haven't heard before."

"In your past?" he asked softly.

"Well, yeah, then, but I still hear things that you wouldn't believe. People come into the restaurant and say all kinds of things."

"Surely not from Pinecraft people."

She shook her head. "No, not from any of the Mennonites or Amish. Mostly just rude outsiders."

"That's terrible. Maybe you should put a sign on the door telling people to leave those things outside." He offered a teasing grin. "Think that'll work?"

She tilted her head back and laughed. "About as well as telling Jeremiah to behave. You know he'll do that again."

"Of course he will. And I'll just have to be ready for him next time."

"What can you do about it?"

Abe shrugged. "I'll search through scripture and come up with some verses to put him in his place in a God-pleasing way."

Mary thought for a few seconds, then nodded and laughed. "If nothing else, he'll stop just to shut you up."

A woman on a three-wheeler bumped up on the lower part of the curb in front of them. Her skirt barely covered her knees, and the ties on her kapp lifted with the breeze. The basket in front of the handlebars was laden with bags from various stores and behind her rolled a wagon filled with jars. The final bump sent a couple of the jars flying off the wagon and crashing onto the sidewalk.

She got off her three-wheeler, extracted a bag from the side of the wagon, and picked up some of the broken pieces. Mary and Abe ran up to her and helped.

"Hello, Abe. Thank you." The woman nodded and darted her gaze toward Mary. Her eyebrows lifted, but she didn't address Mary. "Nice afternoon for a walk." She tucked the bag filled with broken glass into the side of the wagon and hopped back up on her three-wheeler.

"Yes, Mrs. Troyer, it's a very nice afternoon." Abe wanted the woman to acknowledge Mary, but he wasn't sure what he could do to make that happen.

"Looks like you have quite a load there, Mrs. Troyer," Abe said. "Would you like me to take the wagon somewhere for you?"

Mrs. Troyer looked flustered but finally relented and nodded to Abe. "That would be nice. . . ." She tentatively glanced at Mary. "That is, if you don't mind. I'm having a very difficult time."

"No problem at all," he said. "Mary, you don't mind, do you?"

"Of course not."

Abe untied the wagon from the back of the three-wheeler. "We'll follow you." As they fell in behind the woman, with Abe pulling the wagon behind him, he winked at Mary. "As soon as we deliver the load, we'll go get our ice cream."

Mary's opinion of Abe soared even higher. The man was kind to everyone, smart, educated, handsome, and tenacious. To top it off, each time she was with him, the fluttery feelings in her tummy increased.

They arrived at the woman's house, where she hopped off her three-wheeler and pointed to a patch by the door. "Just leave the wagon there. What do I owe you?"

Abe's forehead wrinkled. "Nothing. It was our pleasure."

She grinned. "You are a very sweet man. Thank you." Then she glanced at Mary. "I hope you realize what a fortunate young woman you are to be with a man like Abe."

"I'm the fortunate one for Mary to be with me," Abe said. "If you don't need us anymore, we'll be on our way."

Mary and Abe walked in silence until they came to the end of the block when Mary turned to him. "You didn't have to say anything."

"I know I didn't, but I felt it was the right thing to do."

"I'm used to it, though. In fact, I've come to expect people to think the worst of me."

"That's not right, Mary. Maybe she doesn't think badly of you. Some people simply don't say much."

"Or they want to shun me for what my mother did."

"Mrs. Troyer wasn't shunning you, if that's what you're implying. She is just one of those quiet, shy women. I saw her look at you, and there didn't seem to be any animosity in her eyes."

"So what are you saying, Abe?"

He squeezed his eyes shut for a few seconds as though he might be sending up a brief prayer. Then he looked directly at her. "Perhaps you're the one holding on to the grudge. It's not like your mother was the first to leave the church."

Mary shook her head. "I don't feel like people respect me around here, no matter what I do."

"I think you're a wonderful woman, and I'm sure others do, too." Abe stopped in the middle of the sidewalk and turned her around to face him. "You should never be treated with anything but the utmost respect."

"Thank you." Mary gulped as she looked up into Abe's

eyes, which flickered from the reflection of the afternoon sun. He lowered his head toward her and looked like he was about to kiss her, making her heart hammer so hard she feared Abe would hear it.

But he didn't kiss her. Instead, he took her hand and turned her back around. "I'm hungry for some ice cream. Let's go."

At the moment, Mary didn't care if she never saw ice cream again. She'd much rather have a kiss. Disappointment rolled through her.

When they arrived at the tiny ice-cream shop, Abe asked her what she wanted. "I'll just have whatever you're having." She folded her arms and tried to hide her feelings.

He squinted as though confused by her answer, then turned to the woman behind the counter. "We'll have two double vanilla cones please." After she scooped the ice cream and Abe paid, he handed Mary one cone and licked the other. "Mmm. This is good."

Mary turned her cone around and studied it before tasting it. A tiny drop of ice cream splashed onto her hand, and she licked it off. "Yeah, it is good. Perfect, in fact."

"What just happened back there, Mary?" he asked as they ambled down the street. "You suddenly acted strange."

She paused mid-lick. "Strange? How so?"

"After that conversation when we left Mrs. Troyer, you gave me an odd look. Did I do something wrong?"

"No, Abe," Mary said slowly, wondering if she should leave it at that or explain. "It's just that. . .well. . ."

"You can talk to me about anything, Mary. I want you to trust me."

"Oh I do trust you, Abe." She swallowed deeply and looked down at the sidewalk before meeting his gaze. "Much more than I do most people. It's hard for me, you know."

"Yes," he said as he reached out and brushed a lock of hair

that had escaped her kapp with his free hand. "I do know."

A pinching sensation in her chest and the urge to let Abe know how she felt about him battled with the warning bells going off in her head. Telling him her feelings would leave her vulnerable and exposed. Did she dare do that? She wanted to very badly, but in spite of Abe admitting he was romantically interested in her, the fear of being hurt was still lodged in her heart.

"Mary?" he asked, bending over and tilting her face up to meet his gaze once again. "Talk to me, okay?"

She pulled her lips between her teeth and nodded. Her heart felt as though it would jump out of her mouth if she didn't say something. If ever there was a time to release that fear, this was it. Finally, she sucked in a deep breath, squared her shoulders, looked Abe in the eye, and blurted, "Kiss me, Abe."

seven

Abe blinked, and the ice-cream cone toppled from his hand and fell to the ground. Did Mary just tell him to kiss her? Neh, couldn't have. Not Mary with the standoffish sarcasm and strong-arm defense.

She held her ice-cream cone up with one hand, jammed her other fist on her hips, and leaned forward, lips puckered, eyes narrowed. He had to bite the insides of his cheeks to keep from laughing.

When he didn't do anything, she folded her arms and pouted. "Oh, so you don't wanna kiss me now, huh?"

"Oh I didn't say that. You just caught me by surprise."

"Okay, so do you want to kiss me or not?"

Abe pondered the thought, then slowly nodded. "Yes, I'd love to kiss you, Mary, but not here."

"What's wrong with here?"

"This isn't exactly the best place for us to have our first kiss."

Mary lifted her free hand in surrender. "So you get to pick where we kiss?"

Abe gave himself some time to gather his thoughts before speaking. "Mary, when I kiss you, I want you to understand it's because I have feelings for you. It's not something I take lightly."

"Who said anything about taking it lightly?" She frowned as she took a lick of her ice cream. She shook her head. "Don't tell me you agree with that mean Jeremiah."

"No, this has nothing to do with Jeremiah. What it has everything to do with is letting you know that a kiss means. . . well, it means. . ." He glanced down then back up at her, slowly shaking his head.

Mary lifted an eyebrow in amusement and tapped her foot. "Go on, Abe. I want to know what it means."

"Let's just say it's very special to me. A kiss is not like a handshake or even a hug. It means we're more than just friends."

"I'm okay with that." She held his gaze as though challenging him. "I thought that's what you wanted."

That was exactly what he wanted, but the timing was off. Kissing on command seemed forced and cold. But he didn't want to risk hurting or embarrassing Mary—not after her attempt to be more open and trust him.

"Let's take a little walk, okay?" He extended his elbow, hoping for the best, and to his delight, she took it.

"Sorry about your ice-cream cone," Mary said.

Abe laughed. "I should have held on to it better."

"Want a lick?" she asked, offering her ice-cream cone.

Abe laughed. "No thanks. I'm not about to take your ice cream."

"That's okay, I don't mind. I sort of lost my appetite."

"You don't have to finish it."

They walked in silence for another block then turned up a side street behind some of the small shops at the edge of Pinecraft. Abe pointed to a lonely tree holding court over a tiny patch of grass in the center of a circle of palmettos. "Let's get some shade."

Mary pivoted and headed straight for the tree without a single word. Abe was right behind her. They passed a trash receptacle, and she tossed her dripping ice-cream cone. "I can't eat any more."

Abe leaned against the tree and extended his arms. "Come here, Mary," he said softly.

She took a step toward him then stopped. "Oh, so now you want to kiss me?"

He closed his eyes, retracted his outstretched arms, and

silently chuckled. When he opened his eyes again, she was so close, all he had to do was open his arms and she was in them. "May I kiss you now, Mary Penner?"

She turned her face up to his with her lips puckered and her eyes closed. This time he leaned down and touched her lips with his for a couple of seconds. When he pulled away, she slowly opened her eyes and smiled up at him.

"So that's what a kiss feels like," she said, her voice barely above a whisper. A quick flash of her mother being kissed and groped darted through her mind. A few times men had attempted to touch her, but her quick reflexes and whatever lies she could make up saved her. Mary shuddered as she forced herself to stay in the moment. Abe was nothing like those men, and she knew this was different.

Abe couldn't help but laugh. "Disappointed?"

"Nope. I liked it. Let's do it again." She puckered her lips and closed her eyes.

He dropped a brief kiss on her lips then the tip of her nose. "I think I better get you back before this gets out of control."

"Well," she began slowly as she looked at him coyly. "I have plenty of self-control. It's you I'm worried about."

He chuckled. "I'll be fine."

"Good. Now that we've got that settled, when are we going out again?"

"Now look at you. When I first wanted to get to know you better, you acted like I was the enemy, and now you want to rush things. Why don't we take things nice and slow?"

She shrugged. "What's the point? You like me, and I'm pretty sure I like you."

"You don't mince words, do you, Mary?"

"Why would I do that?"

Her abrupt turnaround both delighted and startled Abe. Something had happened since the last time he'd seen her. "You're acting different now."

"Maybe I am different."

Abe shook his head. "People don't change that quickly. What's going on, Mary?"

"Don't be so skeptical. Nothing's going on, except I've had time to think about us."

"Oh yeah?" He glanced down at her as they walked side by side on the narrow sidewalk. "What were your thoughts?"

"To start with, I know that you're a very nice man, and you seem honest."

"Ya, I like to be nice to people, and honesty comes natural. But plenty of people are nice and honest."

"Oh but not like you, Abe."

He knew some people were puzzled by Mary, and even after all this time, some of them may still have held her past against her. But he hadn't seen anyone being intentionally mean except Jeremiah—even Mrs. Troyer, whose mind seemed to be elsewhere.

"Has anyone said or done anything to hurt you?" he asked. "Besides Jeremiah, that is."

"Not really. I've gotten used to being ignored. But you've never ignored me. You've always acted like I was any other Mennonite girl."

"Trust me," he said with a chuckle. "You're not like any other Mennonite girl."

She gave him a look of pretend hurt then grinned. "I'll take that as a compliment."

"Good. You should." They continued another half block toward her grandparents' house. "It's still not enough to explain why you're suddenly demanding kisses. Why did you ask me for a kiss today?"

Mary contorted her mouth and pondered the thought. Finally she shrugged. "Why not?"

"There you go again, answering my question with a question."

She shrugged. "I wanted a kiss, so I asked for it."

He studied her. "Okay."

"Besides, I like the way I feel when I'm with you."

Now they were getting somewhere. "How do you feel when you're with me?"

"I. . .well. . ." She pursed her lips and sighed. "I think I've already told you too much. Since you want to take things more slowly, I think I'll keep some things to myself."

Abe grinned. "You are such a mystery, Mary Penner."

"Is that a problem?"

"Neh, I think I like it."

"Good. Then my hunch worked out." They'd gotten to the block where her grandparents lived, so she stopped and turned to face him. "Thank you for the ice cream and kiss."

He tilted his head toward her. "And thank you for spending some time with me. . .and the kiss. I'll see you soon."

❧

Mary was pretty sure Abe couldn't see her hands shaking. It had been difficult to hide her nerves, but it was better he didn't know how he affected her. Ever since their lips touched, she felt as though the earth had tilted just enough to throw her off balance.

"Mary, is that you?" Grandma called from the kitchen. Before Mary had a chance to answer, she added, "Come on back and tell me about your ice cream date with Abe."

"I'll be right there, Grandma. I have to put my stuff away first."

As Mary deposited her tote on her bed, she took several deep breaths to get a grip on her nerves and gather some thoughts on what to say about her time with Abe. Maybe Grandma wouldn't ask too many questions.

That hope was quickly shattered when Mary joined her grandmother in the kitchen. "How was your date with Abe?" Before Mary had a chance to say a word, Grandma added,

"You're back awful early. Did something happen?"

Mary reached for the flour canister and moved it to a different spot on the counter so she could help with dinner. "No, nothing happened."

"I thought you'd be home before dinner, but not this early." Grandma pointed to the other canister. "Hand me the sugar, please."

"We got ice cream and went for a walk. That doesn't take very long."

Grandma paused and looked directly at Mary. "You and I need to have a talk. There are obviously some things you don't understand about courting."

Mary's cheeks flamed. "I think I know enough."

"Dating someone you're thinking about spending the rest of your life with involves more than getting ice cream and going for a walk."

"Who said anything about spending the rest of my life with him?"

Grandma shook her head. "Are you saying you're not interested in marrying Abe?"

Mary let out a nervous laugh. "That's not what I'm saying. Things like that take time. Besides, I'm not sure I ever want to get married."

Grandma placed one fist on her hip and shook her other finger at Mary. "Don't ever say that again. If the Lord puts the right man in front of you, who are you to say you don't want to get married?"

Mary knew better than to argue with Grandma about the Lord's will. It would be a losing battle since Grandma knew the Bible front to back. Mary had studied tenaciously since she'd been in Sarasota, but she knew she didn't know scripture like Grandma did.

"I'm not saying you should marry Abe, but don't rule it out. It's not like every Mennonite boy in Sarasota is beating our door down for you." Grandma turned back to the cobbler she'd been working on, leaving Mary to ponder her words.

They sifted, stirred, and rolled dough in silence as Mary's mind wandered from the kiss and Abe's intentions to her motives. Grandma was right. The only man who'd shown any romantic interest in Mary was Abe. If she had her choice, would he be the one she'd pick? Without having the experience, how would she know?

"Mary?" Grandma's voice was soft and tender. "I didn't mean to say you should marry Abe because you can't do better. It's just that your grandpa and I are concerned about you, and Abe is such a nice boy. He's a hard worker, and he has land that would be ideal for a large family."

Grandma and Grandpa had always wanted a dozen children, but Mary knew that for some reason they hadn't been able to have more than one child. Mary couldn't imagine having a houseful of kids underfoot. All the babies and toddlers she'd seen required so much selfless work. And her mother's voice rang through her head. *If I didn't have you to worry about, my life would be so different.*

"I'm not so sure that's what I want," Mary said. "A big family is a lot of work."

"Anything worth having is a lot of work," Grandma replied. "Including Abe."

Mary wanted to end the conversation, so she racked her brain for a new topic. She was about to mention the seasonal crowd at the restaurant when she heard the front door. "Grandpa's home. Eleanor was off today, so he must have left Shelley in charge of closing."

"Hello, ladies," Grandpa bellowed as he entered the kitchen. "Beautiful, sunshiny day."

"Ya." Grandma paused with her hands hovering slightly above the finished cobbler. "Mary got home early from her date with Abe."

Grandpa looked at Mary and winked. "I'm sure she has her reasons."

"Said it didn't take long to eat ice cream."

Mary wished they didn't talk about her as though she weren't there. She wanted to run from the kitchen, but that would make the situation more uncomfortable when she came back.

"She's right," Grandpa said, surprising Mary. "Besides, I think it's a good idea for them to take it easy. We don't want Abe getting the wrong idea, thinking Mary is too eager to find a husband."

"I'm not even looking for a husband," Mary blurted.

Grandma made a clucking sound with her tongue, and Grandpa chuckled. "Good girl. It's harder to find one when you're looking," he said.

"She's not getting younger, Joseph."

He nodded. "I think she knows that. How much longer before supper's ready? I'm starving."

"Not much longer," Mary replied. "The ham and sweet potatoes are ready. As soon as the rolls are done, we can eat."

"In that case, I'll go do some weeding. Let me know when it's time to sit down at the table."

Silence fell between Mary and Grandma after Grandpa left the kitchen. Mary sometimes wondered why Grandpa came home acting as though he might starve to death after working in a restaurant all day. Even though he was surrounded by food, Mary or Shelley sometimes had to remind him to eat lunch. He worked as hard as his employees did, so Mary was more than happy to do what she could to help out at home.

After the rolls came out of the oven, Grandma pointed to the door. "Go let your grandfather know it's time to wash up for supper. Then you can help me put everything on the table."

Mary's skirt swished as she turned around and headed for the back door. She shielded her eyes as she stepped outside on the western side of the house.

Grandpa glanced up. "Supper ready?"

"Yes," she said. "It'll be on the table in a few minutes."

Grandpa nodded. "I'll be there in a moment."

Mary went back inside to help Grandma finish the meal preparation. She sliced the maple-citrus-glazed ham and set it on the table then slid the hot, buttery rolls into the napkin-lined basket. Grandpa liked buttermilk with dinner, so she poured him a glass and set it at the head of the table. Grandma placed a pot holder on the table before putting the dish of sweet potatoes on top of it. The aromas blended and would have had Mary's taste buds on high alert if her stomach wasn't so off-kilter after the afternoon with Abe and the conversation between her grandparents.

"Get the lemonade," Grandma ordered. "I'll get the glasses."

By the time the women had everything laid out, Grandpa appeared. "Have a seat, ladies."

They sat and bowed their heads for the blessing. Mary held her breath as he thanked the Lord for the beautiful day and the food they were blessed with, hoping he wouldn't mention Abe. When he finished with "Amen," she let the air out of her lungs. She opened her eyes to see him staring at her. He winked, and she managed a slight grin in return.

❧

Abe stared at the sandwich on the table. He was getting sick of eating the same old thing every night for supper, but he felt guilty for his dissatisfaction because he never had to go hungry. Although he knew how to prepare a meal, it seemed pointless to go to so much trouble for only one person.

After he and his brothers grew up, his mother mentioned the same thing about cooking for two. "But if I don't prepare a meal for your father, he might wither up and die, then I'd have only myself to cook for."

Abe felt an emptiness in his heart as he longed for the days when his whole family was in the house, eating a lavish dinner prepared by his mother's loving hands. He took a bite of his sandwich and slowly chewed before swallowing and repeating until it was gone.

He carried his plate to the sink, washed it, dried it, and put it away. Next time he went into town, he needed to get something from Penner's to go.

It was still daylight out as he stepped onto the front porch and deeply inhaled the fresh air. The workers had gone home for the day, so here he was, in the middle of his family farm, alone and confused—not only by the way Mary Penner was acting but by how he felt about her. As much as he liked her, he should have been happy to kiss her, but when she ordered him to do it, he was startled.

Then when they finally did kiss, it was even better than he'd expected. He still wondered why Mary had changed toward him so abruptly.

The sound of an automobile turning onto the shell driveway caught his attention, and he turned in the direction of the main road. A bright orange car came barreling toward him. The only person he knew with a car that color was Jeremiah Yoder. Tension rose from his core and extended throughout his entire body. Why would Jeremiah be coming all the way out here?

Abe stepped down off the porch and into the yard. He placed his hands on his hips and glared as the automobile drew closer. He could see Jeremiah's face had a look of determination.

The orange car came to a skidding halt about twenty feet from where Abe stood, and Jeremiah got out. "Hey, Abe. Got a few minutes to chat with an old friend?"

"What are you doing here, Jeremiah?" Abe had to hold back the anger that brewed in his chest.

Jeremiah lifted his hands in surrender. "Hey, man, I just wanted to make amends. I feel bad about what I said in town earlier."

"You do?" This didn't sound like the Jeremiah of late. Abe couldn't help but be suspicious.

"Yep. I was being a class-A jerk, and I'm sorry."

Abe's faith ran deep, and he knew that when a man was sincerely sorry for what he did wrong, he needed to be forgiven. But it wasn't always easy.

"Want some coffee?" Abe asked.

"Nah, I can't drink coffee late in the day or I'll be up all night."

Abe smiled. "Based on what I've heard, being up all night is normal for you these days."

"Yeah, afraid so. But I'm getting older, ya know?"

"I do know. So you've apologized, and you're forgiven." Abe took a step back, hoping Jeremiah would get back into his bright orange car and leave.

"I'd still like to talk"—Jeremiah glanced around—"unless there's something else going on, and you can't."

"Nothing else is going on."

Jeremiah continued standing in the same spot, kicking at the sandy soil beneath his feet, looking uncomfortable while Abe watched and waited. Something was up, and Abe couldn't tell if it was good, bad, or neutral.

"What do you want, Jeremiah?"

Jeremiah shrugged and shook his head but didn't say anything. Instead, he looked everywhere but at Abe. Finally Abe decided someone needed to speak up, so he gestured toward the house. "Do you wanna come inside?"

With a nod, Jeremiah took a step toward the house. Abe led the way in silence, wondering all the way what was so important for Jeremiah to have to talk now.

"Have a seat at the kitchen table," Abe said. "I would offer you something besides coffee, but since I live here alone, I don't generally keep much extra food lying around."

"I didn't come here to eat." Jeremiah pulled out a chair and glanced around before sitting. "This place hasn't changed a bit since we were kids, except for a few missing decorations."

"There's no reason for it to change. I put the decorations away, but I still have them."

"True, there isn't a reason for change." Jeremiah let out a nervous laugh. "But some people like change just for the sake of something different."

"Not me."

"I realize that, and it's the reason I wanted to talk to you."

Abe sat down and leaned back in his chair, arms folded, eyes narrowed. Since he had no idea what Jeremiah wanted to talk about, he didn't know of any questions to ask.

"This isn't easy for me, Abe, so bear with me."

"I'm listening."

"You know I left the church when I realized how much fun I could have." He cleared his throat. "Or how much fun I thought I could have."

"What do you mean by that?"

Jeremiah rolled his eyes upward and looked around the room before settling his attention back on Abe. "It's really strange how enticing the world can be, but when you get smack-dab in the middle of it, there's something not right. It doesn't feel as good as it looks."

"What happened, Jeremiah?"

"Nothing really happened. It's just that I was seeing this girl. Amy. She's very cute and funny and a little bit wild. I knew that, and I was okay with it at first. But the more I got to know her, the more I realized how lost she was. Amy lives for the moment and had the philosophy that if it feels good, it's okay."

Abe never expected to have this kind of conversation with

Jeremiah. He could see the man was troubled, so he nodded his understanding and encouragement to continue.

"Amy's a sweet girl but very misguided. She's been around the block a few times, ya know?"

Abe tilted his head. "Around the block?"

Jeremiah chuckled. "She's been with other men. At first I tried to be cool with it, but as we got deeper into our relationship, I realized how much it bothered me."

"Ya, that would bother most men, I think."

"Not all men, but in spite of the fact that I left the church, my Mennonite roots run deep. I couldn't deal with Amy's wild ways anymore, so I broke it off with her."

"I'm sure that's a very good idea."

Jeremiah tilted his head and gave Abe an odd look. "Don't you worry about that with Mary?"

"Why should I worry about Mary?"

"Well. . ." Jeremiah lifted his hands and let them fall on the table. "You know where she came from, and chances are—"

Abe shot up from his chair. "Don't you ever say another word about Mary's past. She's a good Mennonite girl."

"Okay, okay, I'm just thinking there might be some things you don't know about her. Remember when we first met her? There was some talk about her mother and where she came from and all."

"What happened to Mary was out of her control. She was fourteen when she came here, and since I've known her, she hasn't done anything wrong." Abe's jaw tensed, and he sat back down to try to regain control of his emotions. "Mary is a very sweet woman who is committed to the Lord."

Jeremiah closed his eyes and pursed his lips. He was obviously a very frustrated man.

"I'm still not sure why you came here, Jeremiah," Abe said. "Did you want advice about Amy or to deliver some lies about Mary?"

"Neither."

"Then why are you here?" Abe asked.

Jeremiah sucked in a breath, blew it out, then leveled Abe with a look of determination. "Do you think there's any chance I can come back to the church?"

eight

The next day Mary's nerves were on edge. Each time she heard the bell on the restaurant door, she jumped.

"Expecting someone?" Shelley asked.

"Abe."

Shelley smiled. "I thought so."

"Something must have come up, or he would have been here by now."

"Lunch isn't over yet. Maybe he had some things to do on the farm."

"I'm sure." Another customer walked in and sat down in Mary's section. "At least we're busy today. All these customers are keeping my mind off him."

Shelley laughed. "Who are you trying to fool, Mary? A bomb could explode in the room, and you'd still be thinking about Abe."

Without a response, Mary turned toward her customers. Shelley was right. Nothing would get her mind off Abe—not after that kiss that still had her lips tingling.

After the lunch crowd dwindled, Grandpa approached Mary and handed her the phone. "It's for you," he said.

She answered it with a tentative, "Hello?"

"Is this the Mary Penner who lived in Cincinnati?" The man's voice was barely audible, but it had a familiar tone to it.

Mary's legs nearly gave out, so she lowered herself into the nearest chair. "Who is this?"

The man let out a sinister laugh. "You're good at hiding. It took some work to find you."

"Tell me who you are, or I'm hanging up," Mary demanded.

She heard him laughing as the call disconnected. Whoever that was didn't sound nice at all.

Shelley approached before she had a chance to stand back up. "You okay, Mary?"

Mary blinked and nodded. "That was the strangest phone call. Some man asked me if I was the Mary Penner who lived in Cincinnati, but he didn't tell me who he was or why he wanted to know."

"That truly is strange. Let me know if you need something. I need to check on my customers."

"Thanks." Mary stood and crossed the restaurant to hand the phone back to Grandpa, who was busy filling some late lunch orders. She was glad he didn't have time to talk to her, or he would have asked questions about the call.

At about three thirty, Grandpa walked up and put his arm around her. "Why don't you run on home and tend to the garden so I don't have to."

Grandpa loved his garden, so she suspected he was trying to help get her mind off Abe. She started to say she could stay a little longer, but instead she offered a brief nod. She untied her apron and hung it on the rack.

She was almost to the door when she heard Grandpa call out to her. "Don't rush things, Granddaughter. The Lord knows what's on your heart, and He'll make everything all right."

Mary forced a smile. "Yes, I know that."

"Oh, here, take this to your grandmother," he said as he pulled the last of the cake from the shelf. "I told her you'd bring home whatever dessert was left."

She took the cake, covered it, and went out the back door. After carefully positioning the cake in the basket of her three-wheeler, she hopped on and pedaled home.

Grandma wasn't in the kitchen, so Mary set the cake on the counter and opened the oven door. It was hot, but nothing was in there. *Strange.*

"Grandma, are you home?" she called out. No answer. "Grandma?" She spun around and looked on the message board by the door. Nothing there.

Mary's heart raced. Something wasn't right. She couldn't ever remember a time when Grandma left without telling someone or at least leaving a note. Her head swirled with all kinds of thoughts of what could have happened—particularly after the odd phone call that afternoon. Mary didn't have a cell phone to call Grandpa, so she started to head back to the restaurant. She'd barely mounted her three-wheeler when she spotted the van Abe often rode in when he came to town as it pulled up in front of the house.

Both Abe and Grandma got out. "Where are you off to, Mary?" Grandma asked while Abe went around to the other side of the van and pulled out a big brown box.

"I was—" Mary stopped when the van door slammed. Her jaw dropped, but she quickly recovered and pursed her lips.

Abe carried the box to the curb and set it down before placing his hands on his hips and looking at Grandma. "Where do you want this?"

"By the back door, if you don't mind."

Abe lifted the box and brought it around back while Grandma followed. Mary was right behind them with her three-wheeler.

"Come on inside," Grandma said. "Mary, you can set the table."

Mary glanced back and forth between Grandma and Abe after she placed the dishes on the table. "You weren't here, and I was. . ." Her voice trailed off when she saw the look of amusement on Abe's face. "What's so funny?"

"Nothing," Abe said. "I just think it's sweet that you were worried about your grandmother."

Grandma flicked her hand. "Oh, she wasn't worried about me."

"I was," Mary admitted as relief washed over her. "Did you know you left the oven on?"

"Uh-oh." Grandma made a face. "That's not good."

"I'm afraid it was my fault," Abe said in her defense. "I stopped by and talked her into going with me."

"Where did you go?" Mary asked.

Her grandmother's gaze darted from Abe to Mary. "Abe came by after I got home from the restaurant. We started talking, and next thing I knew, he was taking me out to his farm to show me what he's done."

"Ya," Abe said. "She hadn't been out there since my mother passed away. I wanted her to see how well the citrus was growing."

"Maybe you can go see the farm sometime, Mary. Abe is doing quite well." She bent over the box, opened it, and extracted some of the fruit. "This is from the last of the season's citrus," she explained before turning back to Abe. "I think we can put it to good use around here. Thank you, Abe."

He grinned. "My pleasure, Mrs. Penner."

"You'll be staying for supper, won't you?" Grandma said.

Mary quickly cut her gaze over to Abe, who'd given her a questioning look. He opened his mouth then narrowed his eyes before nodding. "Yes, that would be very nice. I don't normally have a very good supper, so this will be a treat."

"Mary, set an extra place for Abe."

Without a word, Mary did as she was told. Her spirits had been lifted, but she didn't want anyone to notice—particularly not Grandma, who would most likely have something to say about it later.

"Is there anything I can do to help you?" Abe asked.

Grandma shook her head, but Mary pointed toward the back door. "Grandpa asked me to tend his garden, so you can help me out."

"Mary!" Grandma gave her a scolding look. "Abe is a guest!"

"That's all right, Mrs. Penner. I don't mind as long as Mary's with me."

Mary avoided looking directly at Grandma for fear of a reprimanding glare. Instead, she marched straight out to the backyard before turning to face Abe.

"I wondered where you were today when I didn't see you at the restaurant."

Abe grinned. "Do you always worry about people when you don't see them?"

"Who said I was worried? All I said was—"

Abe quickly narrowed the distance between them. He took hold of her gloved hand and held it between both of his, creating a flutter inside her. Mary glanced over toward the window and was relieved not to see Grandma watching. But she pulled her hand back anyway; she didn't want to press her good fortune.

When she glanced back at Abe, she knew he'd seen her look. "I—"

"She knows," Abe said softly. "I told her I wanted to see more of you."

Mary's jaw fell slack again. "And what did she say?"

"I have her blessing. Your grandpa's, too."

"When did you talk to him?" She averted her gaze and bent over to pull a weed from the edge of the garden.

"This morning before you got to the restaurant. I wanted to make sure they understood my intentions before we got too carried away."

Mary shot straight up and planted her weed-filled fist on her hip, then looked directly at Abe. "You didn't tell them I asked for a kiss, did you?"

Abe laughed. "That's the Mary I remember. No, I didn't mention the kiss, but I did say you were spirited and full of surprises."

"Surprises? Me? How about you? So tell me what's going on."

"I want to court you, Mary. I thought I told you I wanted us to get to know each other better."

"You did, but you didn't say anything about courting."

"You're a smart woman. If you thought about it more, you would have figured it out." He lightly touched her cheek then pulled back. "I want to be with you every chance I can."

That was exactly what she wanted, too. But deep down, her mother's words still haunted her, dredging up just enough fear to concern her.

"What if we find out we can't stand each other?" she challenged.

"I doubt that will happen."

"It might. What then?"

He shrugged. "If that's the case, I s'pose we'll know that we're not meant to be together."

That was exactly what Mary was afraid of. But the more she thought about it, she was afraid they *were* meant to be together. And then what? Mary had no idea what to do in a real relationship with a man, and even though she wanted to have a relationship, she feared she wasn't capable of fully trusting him—or any man—with her heart.

She moved faster through the garden, frantically yanking out the spindly, green intruders, tossing them into the bin her grandpa had set by the garden.

"Whoa, there," Abe said. "You're gonna hurt yourself if you keep up this pace. Let me give you a hand." He narrowed his eyes and studied her face. "Is something else going on?"

Mary hesitated but decided to let Abe know about the call. She explained what had happened, and he listened. After she finished, he shook his head.

"That is very strange. I wonder why the man wouldn't tell you his name. Are you frightened?"

"At first I was," she said as she resumed her weeding, going more slowly now that she'd let some of the worry be known. "But I prayed about it, and now I know I'll be fine."

As Abe joined her in weeding, Mary forced herself to calm down. She wanted to believe her fears were uncalled for, but at the moment, they were stronger than her desires.

"God will protect you, but that doesn't mean you have to let down your guard," Abe said. "Please be careful and let people know where you are at all times."

Mary chuckled. "Grandma and Grandpa pretty much know my whereabouts every minute of the day."

"Next time you decide to walk on the beach, you might want to have someone go with you." He grinned. "I'll be glad to volunteer."

"I'm sure." She smiled back at Abe.

"Mary."

She glanced up toward the sound of her grandfather's voice. "I got a late start, but Abe's helping me, so I'm almost done."

"You don't have to do any more, Mary. I didn't intend for you to put our guest to work."

Abe straightened. "She didn't put me to work, Mr. Penner. I insisted."

"That's fine, but come on inside. You're our guest, and I want you to feel welcome. Sarah told me you gave us some fruit. We should be weeding your garden, not the other way around."

Abe grinned. "I don't expect anything in return."

Grandpa gave a clipped nod. "I understand, but both of you, come on into the house and wash up for supper."

Mary tossed the last of the weeds into the bin then removed her work gloves. She dropped them on the table on the back porch. Abe was right behind her.

After they washed up for supper, Mary helped Grandma finish getting the food on the table. They all sat down and joined hands.

Grandpa said the blessing. He gave Mary's hand a squeeze before letting go. "This looks delicious, Sarah."

Grandma made a clucking sound with her tongue. "I know what you like to eat."

Conversation was all about the food, which suited Mary just fine. She didn't feel like answering personal questions—particularly with Abe sitting right across from her. And she was glad he didn't bring up the phone call.

"This is good, Mrs. Penner," Abe said. "I haven't had a meal like this in. . .well, since my mother died."

Grandpa held his fork midair as he gave Abe a comical look. "Not even at the restaurant? We like to think the food there is as good as home cooking."

Abe chuckled. "Well, other than the restaurant. I should have clarified."

"That's okay, Abe," Grandpa said as he belted out a laugh. "I was just teasing. My Sarah is the best cook in Sarasota, and no restaurant food can even come close."

"Mary is a good cook, too," Grandma added. "I've been teaching her."

"Maybe I'll have the pleasure of eating something she cooks sometime," Abe said as he stabbed another bite with his fork. He cast a quick glance in Mary's direction, and she saw the humor in his eyes.

Grandma lifted her eyebrows and exchanged a glance with Grandpa, and neither of them said a word. The idea of cooking for Abe was pleasant, but an awkward silence hung in the air.

❧

After Abe got home, he pondered the conversation while they were weeding and how different she was during supper. He sensed that Mary was worried about the call, but he couldn't imagine anything happening to her in Pinecraft.

Mary didn't say much during the meal, particularly after

his comment about her cooking something for him. Her sensitivities were different from most people's. Abe suspected it had everything to do with her past. Until he could get her to open up more and talk about it, he'd never know what happened to make her so skittish. Her scars ran deep, and he knew that until she faced her past, it would forever darken her world. He decided to back off and stop trying so hard to court Mary. If it turned out to be the Lord's will, she would come around naturally, but at the moment Abe didn't see that happening.

The day had been long and tiring, so Abe didn't have any trouble sleeping. He awoke the next morning to the sound of someone banging on his front door. He opened it and found himself looking at a middle-aged man he'd never seen before.

"I'm Jonathan Polk," the man said. "David said you were looking for workers, and I need a job."

"Can you give me a few minutes?" Abe asked.

"Sure. If you don't mind, I'll wander around and take a look-see at your land."

Abe went to his room and dressed then to the kitchen to make some coffee. When he went back outside with two mugs of coffee, Jonathan was standing by the split-rail fence, looking out over the property.

"Nice place you have here," Jonathan said as he took the mug.

"Ya. I like it."

"How long have you been farming in Florida?"

"All my life." Abe sipped his coffee. "I'm the third generation. My father moved here with his parents and started a celery farm. Have you ever worked on a farm?"

Jonathan slowly shook his head. "No, but I've worked with my hands plenty, I'm handy with machines, and I learn quickly."

"I can't pay a big salary."

"That's fine," Jonathan said. "I'll just be happy to have regular work."

Abe nodded his understanding. At least the man was looking for work—not handouts.

"If I hire you, I'll need you to learn all aspects of farming. We work hard, and we don't specialize in any one thing around here."

Jonathan turned away from Abe and looked out over the farm again before speaking. "There's something refreshing about working hard outdoors. Even though the only outside work I've ever done has been yard work at home, I think it would be good for me." He paused before adding, "And for you. I'm honest, reliable, and loyal. I'm pretty good at fixing things."

Abe needed someone soon, and he hadn't been able to find any Mennonite workers. Jonathan sounded like a man of integrity, plus he'd been referred by David, who knew what Abe needed.

"Can you start tomorrow?" Abe asked.

Abe could tell it took a few seconds before the question registered with Jonathan. Suddenly he grinned. "You mean it? I'm hired?"

"Ya. Come back tomorrow, and I'll start teaching you all about dairy farming."

They walked toward Jonathan's car, where he handed Abe his mug. "What time do you want me here in the morning?"

"Six thirty." Abe thought for a few seconds before correcting himself. "Make that six. I'll need to show you a few things to get you started."

Jonathan nodded. "I'll be here earlier than that if you need me."

"No need to be earlier. Six is just fine."

Abe stood with both mugs in his hands as he watched Jonathan pull away from the house. After the car disappeared from sight, he headed inside to wash the mugs and get ready to go to town. David was supposed to pick him up at nine, and he'd overslept. He'd spent a good hour chatting with Jonathan, touring the farm, and discussing cows and citrus, and it was already a quarter to eight.

❧

Mary had just served a large party of ten when she spotted Abe walking through the restaurant door. Grandpa pointed toward her and said something to him.

Her heart fluttered as Abe got closer, but she forced herself to glance away. She took her time making her way to him. He'd turned down the menu enough times she knew he didn't need one.

"What would you like this morning, Abe?" She had to take a deep breath in order to steady her nerves and keep her hand from shaking as she held the pen above the order pad.

"What do you think would be good for me?" he asked with a teasing tone.

"It's up to you. Would you like a boiled egg, oatmeal, and some fruit, or do you prefer ham, eggs, and fried potatoes?" She scrunched her nose as she finished the question.

Abe leaned back, folded his arms, and smiled as their gazes met. "I'll take the healthy breakfast. . .that is, if it makes you happy."

She tried to keep her emotional balance as she jotted that down on the pad and stepped away. "Good choice," she said as she left and walked toward the kitchen.

"You look good when your eyes twinkle," Shelley said.

"I have no idea what you're talking about." Mary refused to look directly at Shelley, who was obviously having some fun.

"Don't tell me you don't know how much you light up whenever Abe's around."

"He's just another customer." Mary couldn't prevent the grin that tweaked her lips.

Grandpa chose that moment to round the corner and walk toward them. "I'm glad Abe is here. I was beginning to wonder when he'd come back after he said he wanted to court you."

Mary kept her focus on her task. "He's just hungry."

She heard Shelley snicker as she brushed past to get the next order up.

Abe's food was ready a couple of minutes later. Shelley had returned to the kitchen, and she gestured toward Mary's kapp. "You might want to straighten up a bit before you go back out there."

"I'm fine," Mary said, determined not to do anything different just because Abe was there. If he wanted to get to know her better, he might as well get used to the fact that her kapp was often at an angle. Even after all this practice, she still struggled with getting it just right on her head.

She pulled the plates from the counter and carried them to Abe. "Here's your fruit," she said as she placed the bowl filled with strawberries, blueberries, and cantaloupe in front of him. "Be careful with the oatmeal." She put that down beside the fruit bowl. "It's very hot. I'll have your boiled eggs right out."

"No hurry," he said. "Are you able to take a break and join me?"

Mary quickly shook her head and spun around to get the rest of his meal when a little boy running past tripped her. Embarrassment flooded her when suddenly she felt herself being scooped up by a firm, strong arm.

"Whoa there, Mary." Abe caught her and set her back on her feet. "You okay?"

She took the opportunity to straighten her kapp and run her hands down the sides of her full skirt. "I'm just fine. Thank you for catching me. . .again."

"Children need to be taught manners before they're

allowed out," Abe said. "When I have my own, that's one of the first things I'll teach them."

"I—I'm sure you will." Mary allowed a brief sidelong glance in Abe's direction before she scurried toward the kitchen again.

"If Abe hadn't been there, you might have been hurt." Shelley handed Mary a glass of water. "You've been working so hard, Mary. Why don't you sit down for a little while? I can handle the crowd."

"I can't do that to you, Shelley. I'm fine."

Grandpa handed Abe's boiled eggs to Mary. "Take these over to Abe and have a seat at his table." He leveled her with a firm gaze. "I'll bring you something to eat."

"I—"

He tilted his head forward and gave her an even sterner look she couldn't argue with. She carried Abe's eggs to him. "Is the offer still open to join you?"

Abe gestured to the seat across from him. "Ya. I'd be honored for you to sit down with me."

Mary had only been seated about a minute before Grandpa came over with a cup of coffee and a bowl of fruit for her. "Would you like some oatmeal?"

She nodded. "Yes, please."

"I'll have Shelley bring you some. Why don't you relax for a while and enjoy Abe's company? I'm sure Abe wouldn't mind, right?"

"I would love that, but I can't stay long. I have a new worker coming out to the farm tomorrow, and I have to get everything ready for him."

Grandpa seemed pleased. "It's nice to hear that you're doing well enough to hire more people. Isn't that right, Mary?"

"Yes." She fidgeted with the napkin in front of her.

"Shelley will be right over with your oatmeal." Grandpa

turned and headed back to the kitchen to turn in her order.

"You seem rather glum today, Mary." Abe cracked his egg and began to peel it.

Mary didn't know what to say. Her crazy, mixed-up feelings for Abe were enough to send her to the funny farm, as Mama used to tell her. "I'm not glum."

"Good. I was worried I might have said or done something to upset you."

"No, you've been very kind, Abe."

He put down the peeled egg, placed his forearms on the table, and leaned toward her. "Then what is going on? Just when I thought we were getting along—as friends, of course—you started acting strange."

nine

Abe watched Mary as she fidgeted with the napkin. All sorts of thoughts flowed through his mind.

"Do you want me to leave you alone?" he asked. "You're confusing me, Mary. I tried very hard to show you how much I care, and I think you know I'm willing to be your friend even if you don't want more."

Mary's gaze locked with his. She slowly shook her head. "No, Abe, that's not what I want. I guess I'm just skittish because I never understood why you would want to court me in the first place. Surely you could do much better than me."

"I don't know about that." He sighed. Mary's tight grip on her past still frustrated him. "There isn't any reason, besides the fact that I like you, Mary—very much."

"But why?" She tilted her head and gave him a look that broke his heart.

"Why wouldn't I? You seem faithful to the Lord and to the people you love. I always see you in church, praying and helping others. The look on your face when you worship is pure. You never fail to do whatever your grandparents need you to do. You're sweet beneath that shell you use to hide your heart."

Her eyes fluttered closed, then they instantly widened, sending a bolt of shock through him. There was something else between him and Mary—something he couldn't explain because even he didn't understand it.

"Why do you pay so much attention to me in order to know all this?" she asked. "What have I done to deserve your attention?"

Abe lifted his hands in surrender. "I have no idea. Maybe it's just a feeling I have."

"There are some things. . ." She met his gaze as he lifted one eyebrow. "Some things you don't know about my past."

When she stopped talking, he urged her to continue. "I'm willing to listen if you want to tell me, but I doubt there's anything that will make me change my mind."

"I saw some very bad things before I came here, Abe." She lowered her head as if in shame. "Bad things I can't talk about to anyone. I suspect no one in this community has ever experienced what I did at a very young age."

Abe reached across the table and placed his hand over hers. "That was something you couldn't help, Mary. And I believe others here might have had some bad experiences they don't talk about, too. I want you to trust me."

"I'm not completely blameless, either. I lied my way through life many times."

"You were a child, Mary. You did what you thought you had to do. No one is holding that against you."

"Maybe you're right."

"Even if you don't want more than friendship, I still want you to trust me."

Mary licked her lips and looked him in the eye. "I want to trust you, too."

Abe took a deep breath, glanced around the room, then turned back to Mary and exhaled. "The Lord brought you here nine years ago, and I felt something then, but I was too young to know what to do. After all that time, I aimed to find out if I was in His plan to be a part of your life, now that we're adults. I've never been interested in any woman besides you, Mary. I wanted to get to know all about you and what makes you the person you are."

A tiny smile tweaked the corners of her lips. She put down the napkin she'd shredded.

"I'm very happy to be with you, but I don't understand so many things about myself, I can't imagine you ever figuring them out."

"Oh, but I'm willing to try." Abe didn't add the fact that her challenging ways intrigued him even more. He didn't want to say anything that might be misconstrued. "As a friend, of course." Abe still wanted more, but he knew it was out of his hands.

Shelley arrived and placed a bowl of oatmeal in front of Mary. "Topped with brown sugar and apples, just the way you like it."

"Thank you, Shelley."

After Shelley left, Abe leaned forward and inhaled the aroma wafting from Mary's bowl. "That smells delicious."

"It is." Mary lifted her spoon and swirled the fruit into the cereal. "Mama used to eat her oatmeal this way." She closed her eyes to say a quiet blessing.

Abe studied her face until she opened her eyes. "You don't talk much about your mother, Mary. I'd like to know more about her."

She frowned. "Like what? If all the rumors about her are true?"

"No, I'm sure most of the rumors are just that. Rumors. But I would like to know what the two of you did together and where you lived."

Mary shrugged. "Mama and I mostly just found ways to survive. After she left here at sixteen, she didn't know what to do. At least that's what she told me later. It wasn't easy, being a teenage mother with no one to help her."

"I'm sure."

They sat in silence as Mary lifted a spoon half filled with oatmeal to her mouth. Abe didn't want to push, but she'd told him just enough to create more questions in his mind.

"What?" she asked after her next bite. "Why are you

looking at me like that?"

This obviously wasn't a good time to ask questions. "I'm sorry if I upset you. It's just difficult for me to know what to say to you sometimes."

"Maybe it's best not to say anything." She put her spoon into the bowl and stood up. "I better be getting back to work now. I've taken enough time off already."

Abe stood until she left, then he sank back down into his seat. Just when he thought he'd made a step forward, he said or did something that made him slide back. If he didn't feel called by God to continue, he would consider backing down. But every time he thought he might be better off with someone else, something happened to pull him back in Mary's direction. The memory of Mary demanding a kiss brought a smile to his face and joy to his heart.

&

Mary managed to finish her shift without crying, but it hadn't been easy. After Abe brought up her mother, that familiar lump formed in her throat, and she wanted to run out of the restaurant and hide.

As sweet as Abe had been to her, Mary couldn't push her mother's words from her mind. If she hadn't seen her grandmother's anger firsthand, she might have thought her mother's words were childish rebellion. But after Mary moved in with Grandma and Grandpa, she'd overheard some conversations between them that made her think she wasn't wanted. Their talks late at night when they thought she wasn't listening used to worry her, but she eventually became numb to comments about how unexpected her arrival had been and how difficult it was to raise a child at their age. Mary felt secure as long as she stayed on their good side, and now she wondered if Grandma and Grandpa had taken her in to try to redo the mistakes they'd made in the past.

Mama's stories continued to haunt her. She sensed that the

only man her mother ever trusted was Grandpa, and even that trust had been shaken when he hadn't protected her from everyone's wrath.

Instead of going home after work, Mary took the bus back to the beach. She decided she'd walk along the water rather than sit this time.

The beach was even more crowded with tourists. "Hey, Mommy," she heard a little girl say. "Why is that lady dressed like that?" Her mother's reply was in a hushed tone, and Mary couldn't make out what the woman said.

Most of the locals were used to seeing Mennonites around town, but many of the tourists weren't accustomed to their presence. She wanted to be invisible, but with her kapp and long, full skirt, that was impossible. What if she secretly changed into Yankee clothes once in a while, just to hide from the world? The irony of shedding clothes in order to hide gave her a chuckle.

Half expecting to hear Abe's voice behind her caused her to glance over her shoulder every once in a while. But she didn't. All she heard were the sounds of water washing up on the beach, birds calling out to each other, and the high-pitched sounds of kids playing.

The sun was hotter than last time, so she didn't stay on the beach long. After a brief walk, she went back to the bus stop and waited. The flurry of emotions continued swirling around her, escalating her confusion. She no longer fit into the outside world, but she'd never felt like she fully belonged in the Mennonite community. She felt like a misfit, no matter where she was.

She boarded the bus after it stopped. No one else was on it, so she took a seat toward the front. Mary felt very alone.

A few stops later, Mary got off the bus a block from the restaurant. In order not to be seen, she darted between buildings and went straight around back to get her three-wheeler. She was about to take off when the sound of someone sniffling caught her attention.

Mary glanced over her shoulder and saw Shelley by the garbage cans behind the restaurant, dabbing her eyes, her body racked with sobs. She hopped off the three-wheeler and ran over to her friend and coworker.

"What happened, Shelley? Was a customer mean to you?"

Shelley stiffened as Mary gripped her arm. She looked up to Mary with red-rimmed eyes and shook her head. "Peter told me he's marrying Clara."

"But I thought—" Mary stopped herself before blurting that she thought Peter was about to propose to Shelley. "Clara who?"

Shelley sniffled again and blew her nose. She cleared her throat. "Clara from Pennsylvania."

"Do we know her?" Mary asked.

Shelley shook her head. "I saw her talking to Peter once, but I just thought they were acquaintances."

"How can he do that, after courting you for so long?"

"He said he and I were just very good friends all along and that I should be happy for him. I feel so stupid now."

"Join the club," Mary said. "I feel that way most of the time."

"I thought I did everything right. Whenever he wanted to do something, I was always right there, willing to do it with him. When he needed help with the food drive, I jumped in and volunteered. At the potlucks, he always wanted to sit with me, so I saved him a place. Wanna know what he asked me to do?"

Mary shook her head. "No telling."

"He wants me to be in charge of the food for his wedding."

"Peter isn't as smart as I thought he was."

"No, Mary, I think I'm the one who isn't very smart. Now that I think back, I can't remember a time when Peter ever said anything about getting married."

"Didn't he tell you he loved you?"

Shelley shook her head. "Never. Not even once. All he said was that we were about as close as two people could get without being husband and wife. I read into it too much."

"Everyone thought you two would get married."

"I know. He said something else I didn't expect. He told me he always felt sorry for me because of William."

Mary gasped. "William is so sweet and such a blessing."

"Yes, I know. I thought Peter understood that, too. But he's just like the rest of the people we knew in school, even though he's a couple years older."

Mary dropped her arms by her sides. This just validated her mother's words about men even more. Even from her vantage point, Peter had appeared smitten with Shelley. When they were at church, he never let Shelley out of his sight. He even came to the restaurant asking where his girl was.

"This is terrible, Shelley, but you're a strong woman. You can stand up to him and show you're not the least bit fazed by his silliness and. . ." She wanted to say *stupidity*, but she held back. She'd already said enough.

Shelley let out a tiny half giggle/half sob. "Mary, you are such a good friend. I'm glad you came back when you did." She blew her nose then stuffed the tissue back into her pocket. "By the way, where did you go? Your grandfather said you left, but when I came out here, I saw your wheels."

"Sometimes when I need to think I catch the bus and go to the beach." Mary tugged Shelley away from the spot where she'd been standing. "Why don't you come to my grandparents' house with me? I'm sure Grandma wouldn't mind you staying for supper."

"No, I have to cook for William. Our parents are up in Ohio visiting family." Shelley took hold of Mary's hand. "Thank you for caring. I don't know what I would have done if you hadn't come along when you did."

"You would have done the same thing for me," Mary said. "In fact, you have. Sometimes when I feel lost or all alone, you say something or give me a look that lets me know I'm not."

Shelley squeezed Mary's hand then let go. "I need to get on home now. William is probably worried about me."

"Tell William I said hi." Mary hopped back up on the seat of her three-wheeler. "Speaking of worry, I need to get home and help Grandma with her chores. I don't want her to worry about me."

On the way home, Mary thought about the similarities between her life and Shelley's. Although Shelley had never left the community, her older brother had fallen away from the church and her younger brother had Down syndrome, which made some of the other kids in school very uncomfortable. At first Mary wondered why Shelley was such a loner, but after she went home with Shelley a few times, she learned.

Sometimes life just didn't seem fair. Mary had done nothing to cause other people to pretend she didn't exist, yet some still did.

Mary's mother had shared her faith with Mary, but she always mentioned the inconsistencies she'd noticed from some of the people who attended church. Not all of them, but some had twisted the Gospel to fit their agenda.

Shelley somehow maintained her sweetness, and her zest for everything she did gave her the ability to overlook other people's pitying glances. She was the only person who'd actually gone out of her way to be nice to Mary. Perhaps she understood how Mary felt on some level.

What Peter had done was incomprehensible. As Mary reflected on how much time Shelley had put into that relationship, she had no doubt Peter had strung Shelley along, knowing what she expected. Mary knew she wasn't supposed to be angry. The Lord would want her to turn her anger over to Him and simply pray His will be done. It wasn't easy, but as soon as she pulled into her grandparents' yard, that was exactly what she did. Mary had just closed her eyes and begun to speak to the Lord, asking for help in knowing how to comfort Shelley, when she heard Grandma.

"Mary, is that you? Come inside right now. I need you to give me a hand in here."

"I'll be right there," Mary called back. She closed her eyes again, finished her prayer, and said "Amen" aloud before hopping off her three-wheeler and going inside to see what Grandma wanted.

"Grace Hoffstetter is sick, and her husband, Bernard, needs some supper. I fixed them a little something, but I can't leave the house. I want you to take this over to them." She pointed to a casserole cooling on the counter. "You can stop by the restaurant and see if there's any pie left from today that you can take with you. Tell your grandfather I said it was okay."

Mary nodded. Grandpa wouldn't have minded if she'd taken pie, even if Grandma hadn't said anything, but she didn't need to mention that. "Is it just for Mr. Hoffstetter?" Mary asked.

"As far as I know. I don't think Grace can eat yet." A pinched look came over Grandma's face. "Josephine still hasn't returned."

Mary had overheard Grandma telling Grandpa about Josephine Hoffstetter leaving the church. No doubt it brought back haunting memories of their own earlier lives.

As Mary and Grandma got a basket loaded with some bread and other items to take with the casserole, Mary tried to make conversation. "What's wrong with Mrs. Hoffstetter?"

"Don't know exactly."

"Is it serious?"

"Don't think so."

Grandma's clipped words let Mary know she wasn't in the mood to talk. They finished packing the food in silence.

"Don't stop anywhere except the restaurant," Grandma said. "I want this food to still be warm when you get to the Hoffstetters'."

Mary bit her bottom lip. Grandma still treated her like she didn't have the sense to know what she needed to do.

After everything was all packed up, Grandma touched Mary's arm, stopping her. "Your grandfather and I have been talking. We think it's time for you to get a cell phone so you can let us know where you are."

"I can just tell you where I'm going," Mary said. "I don't need a cell phone."

"We'd like for you to have one, even if it's on one of those prepaid plans. You make plenty of money in tips, and you don't have anything else to spend your money on."

"I'll think about it," Mary said. "Let me get this to the Hoffstetters now so I can be back in time to help out with our supper."

Grandma nodded. "You are right, Mary. We don't need to worry about you." Her expression softened. "I will give you credit for being a good girl. . .at least so far."

Stunned, Mary lifted her eyebrows. "I try to be."

"Now go on, get outta here. I'm sure Bernard is half-starving by now." Grandma shooed her out the door.

After carefully placing the casserole and other items in the basket, Mary got on her three-wheeler and pedaled toward the restaurant to pick up some dessert for the Hoffstetters. She'd turned the last corner near the restaurant when she caught a glimpse of Abe bent over a car, talking to someone through the side window. He obviously didn't see her, so she scooted around back.

She found a safe spot for her three-wheeler, secured it, and walked into the restaurant, where Grandpa was finishing the late afternoon cleanup. "Grandma told me to pick up some dessert for the Hoffstetters. Got anything good?"

"Ya." He pointed toward the pie case. "Take your pick. Give them enough for tomorrow, too."

Mary found a couple of to-go containers and carefully placed some chocolate cream pie in one and some coconut cake in the other. As she left, she lifted her hand in a wave. "See you in a little while."

"Does your grandmother want me to bring something home?" he asked.

"She didn't say, but I'm sure that would be good."

He nodded. "Okay, I'll bring some cornbread and the rest of the chocolate pie—that is, if you left any."

"Oh there's plenty left," Mary said. She shoved the door open with her backside and slipped out.

She couldn't help but look for Abe when she got outside, but she didn't see him. That was just as well. She needed to get this food to the Hoffstetters and then head straight home to help Grandma.

It was a gorgeous day, with a blue sky and a few fluffy clouds that had drifted in from the Gulf of Mexico. A couple of seagulls called out as they flew over. The palm trees lining both sides of the road completed the postcard-perfect setting. The gentle breeze lifted the hair that had fallen beneath her kapp and fluttered the leaves of the trees.

Mary sighed. She was blessed to be here in Sarasota, even though memories continued to haunt her. Grandma's occasional softening gave her hope, but it rarely lasted long. She knew it was time to let go of her past and allow herself to appreciate God's blessings and forgive anyone who chose to treat her poorly, but it was harder than simply making the decision to do it.

After Mary made sure both of the Hoffstetters were fed and comfortable and the dishes were washed, she left their house. She'd turned the corner past the restaurant when she spotted Abe getting out of the car she'd seen him standing beside earlier. She was about to call out to him when the driver's side door opened and out stepped Jeremiah. It wasn't the same car she'd seen Jeremiah in earlier.

Alarm bells rang in Mary's head. What was Abe doing with Jeremiah?

ten

Mary's heart lurched as she saw Abe and Jeremiah talking and laughing together as though they were good friends. Jeremiah stepped beside Abe on the sidewalk, and they went off in the other direction.

She stopped pedaling and tried to process what she'd just seen. All this time Abe had seemed appalled by Jeremiah's behavior and the things he'd said. Now, however, he looked perfectly fine with the man who'd fallen away from the church and said those horrible words about her.

Mary's mother's words drifted back into her mind. During the past several days, Mary had convinced herself that Abe was different and that he was the one man besides Grandpa who could be trusted. Now she doubted herself and her ability to discern anything about anyone.

She began pedaling as fast as she could, dodging people on the sidewalk as she headed home. By the time she arrived, she was hot and sweaty, and her face flamed.

Grandpa had obviously just arrived home. He stood not far from the kitchen door, smiling, but she didn't bother saying a word as she brushed past him.

"Mary!" Grandma's voice echoed through the tiny house. "Come here right now. Don't you just tear through the house like a spoiled child. What happened?"

Mary could hear Grandma getting closer. She was tempted to close her bedroom door, but that would only make the problem worse.

Grandma stopped in the bedroom doorway and glared at her. "What's got you in such a dither?"

Mary slowly shook her head. "Nothing that matters."

"If it doesn't matter, then I need you to come help me in the kitchen. I've been waiting for you. I expected you home a while ago. You were supposed to drop off the food and come right back."

"Mr. Hoffstetter said his wife might eat a little if I took it to her, so I did. Then she asked me to make some lemonade with some lemons Abe dropped off earlier, and—"

"Stop." Grandma held up her hand. "I get the picture. You helped the Hoffstetters, which was the right thing to do. Now let's get moving so we can get supper done with before it gets dark." She issued a stern look before going back to the kitchen.

Mary sucked in a deep breath and slowly blew it out. She hoped she could get through the evening without losing her composure. Until seeing Abe, she hadn't realized just how much she'd begun to think something might work out between them. He'd made it clear he wanted to advance their relationship, and it was starting to sound mighty good. But now that he was buddying up with Jeremiah, there was no way she could trust him.

The tiny houses rented by the Mennonite and Amish families in Pinecraft were wired for electricity, so most of them, even those from the Old Order, used it sparingly. But Grandma and Grandpa preferred not to any more than necessary, which was why they tried to eat dinner before it got dark. They occasionally used candles, but with the large picture window across the back of the wall in the kitchen, it generally wasn't necessary.

Mary went into the bathroom and splashed water on her face, hoping to cool off. By the time she joined Grandma in the kitchen, she was able to think more rationally. Grandpa was out in the backyard, surveying his tiny garden.

"Crumble up that sleeve of crackers, Mary, and sprinkle

them over the casserole. We can stick it back in the oven for a few minutes and have a nice crust." Grandma stirred something on the stove then turned down the burner. "Oh, by the way, we're having company for supper, so you'll need to set an extra place."

"Company?" Mary asked. "Who?"

Grandma's lips twitched into a smile. "Abe."

Mary's arm stilled, and her ears rang. "Abe is coming over for supper?"

"Ya. Your grandfather saw him after closing the restaurant, and he invited him to come eat with us. I thought you'd like that."

What could Mary say? She forced herself to continue preparing the cracker-crumb topping for the casserole.

"We have a special key lime pie for dessert. I thought that would be nice to serve company," Grandma said.

"Yes, it's very nice."

"Mary, turn around and look at me."

Slowly, Mary did as she was told. She tried hard to wipe any expression from her face, but she didn't think she succeeded.

"What are you so unhappy about?"

"Nothing. It's just that I enjoy spending time with you and Grandpa—just the three of us."

Grandma scowled. "Stop being selfish. Abe goes home to an empty house every night. He appreciates having a good meal with a family. Maybe someday soon he'll have a wife and then a family of his own." The harshness on Grandma's face softened.

"Maybe." Mary couldn't tell Grandma about the shock and the emptiness in her heart after seeing Abe with Jeremiah. She wouldn't understand.

ஒ

Not much surprised Abe, but when Jeremiah had come to

his house and asked what he could do to get back into the church, he was taken aback—particularly after the comments Jeremiah had shouted from his car. When Abe cornered him about that, Jeremiah seemed sincerely sorry for acting out in such a childish way.

"I guess I've formed some bad habits that I'll have to break," Jeremiah had explained.

"Ya, I guess you have."

Jeremiah had talked for more than an hour about his life outside the church. He said it was fun at first. Someone gave him a job, and shortly after that he'd learned to drive. When he had enough money saved, he bought his automobile. With the freedom of his own wheels came some things he said he was ashamed of.

"I don't think I need to go into the details," he admitted, "but I can tell you it's not anything that made me a better man."

Abe asked why he wanted to come back to the church if being on the outside was so much fun. The look of anguish on Jeremiah's face touched Abe.

"It's really not as much fun as I originally thought. There's a lot of trouble and insecurity in this world."

"Ya. There is that, but you won't be able to completely get away from it. Even if you come back to the church, you might still see it."

Jeremiah folded his hands on the table. "The difference is with the church, you know there's hope."

"Have you prayed about this?" Abe asked.

"I tried. But it felt awkward."

Abe led Jeremiah in prayer then told him it was time to go see someone from church who could counsel him. But first he had some work to do on the farm. Jeremiah offered to help. After they finished, they went back into town to see one of the church elders.

The initial meeting with Franz Bartel, the church elder, had gone much better than Abe had expected. In fact, Franz said the folks at the church had been praying for Jeremiah.

"But I hope you understand that we must be very cautious about proceeding," Franz had explained. "We don't want our members to think we have a revolving door that you can come and go through on a whim."

"Yes," Jeremiah said as he hung his head. "I understand."

"Are you willing to answer questions?" Franz asked. "Some of them may be quite personal, but we want you to repent of all the sins you've committed during this. . .extended rumspringa."

Jeremiah nodded, but the pain on his face was evident. Abe didn't feel sorry for him, though, because he'd made the choice while others remained faithful to God.

After they left the Bartels' house, Abe asked Jeremiah if he'd like to have some coffee at Penner's Restaurant. "They shouldn't be crowded since it's still about an hour before people arrive for dinner."

"Sounds good," Jeremiah said. "I can take you back home afterward."

As soon as they walked into the restaurant, Joseph Penner greeted Abe but gave Jeremiah a curious look. When Jeremiah got up to use the men's room, Joseph made a beeline for Abe's table and asked what was going on. Abe explained Jeremiah's desire to return to the church.

"Praise the Lord," Joseph said, "but be very careful. The serpent knows the Gospel as well as you and I do, and he's not afraid to use it to his advantage."

"Ya, that I do know," Abe agreed. "Mr. Bartel already explained that it will take some time for people to accept him back."

"Would you like to join my family for supper tonight?"

Abe wanted to jump at the offer, but he still needed a ride

home, and he wasn't sure David was available. Before he replied, Jeremiah came back to the table.

"Hello, Mr. Penner. Good to see you again."

"Ya, son, it's been a very long time." Joseph placed a hand on Jeremiah's shoulder. "I'm happy to see you, too."

Abe cleared his throat. "I have a special favor, Jeremiah. Would you mind picking me up at the Penners' after supper?"

"Or you may join us for supper, if you like," Joseph added. "Sarah and Mary always make plenty of food."

Jeremiah grinned. "I think it would be best if I didn't surprise Mary just yet, so I'll take a pass on supper. But I'll be glad to pick you up afterward, Abe. What time?"

Abe glanced at Joseph, who shrugged, then he turned back to Jeremiah. "Mind if I call you?"

"Sure, that's fine."

Joseph left the table. Shelley stopped by to refill their coffee. At first she didn't look Jeremiah in the eye, but then Abe mentioned that Jeremiah was trying to come back to the church.

"That's nice," she said.

To Abe's surprise, Jeremiah spoke up. "I heard about what happened with Peter. He made a very big mistake."

Shelley gasped. "I. . .uh. . ."

"I'm sorry," Jeremiah said. "I guess I shouldn't have been so direct. It's just that I always thought you were very sweet." He paused before adding, "And I. . .when we were younger, I wanted to be your boyfriend."

After Shelley recovered from shock, with cheeks still tinged pink, she smiled at Jeremiah. "Thank you." She held up the pot of coffee. "I'll check on you in a little while, in case you want more coffee."

Abe's heart went out to Shelley. Even he was surprised at Jeremiah's audacity to be so outspoken about his childhood feelings. "I think we've had enough coffee."

After she left, Abe snickered. "Did you mean what you just told Shelley?"

"Absolutely. In fact, one of the reasons I went so wild was from jealousy of Peter. I never could understand what she liked about him."

"You can't blame someone else for your indiscretions, Jeremiah."

"Yes, I'm aware of that. What I did was my own fault."

After they finished their coffee, Abe paid Joseph on their way out. Abe and Jeremiah went out to the parking lot. "Mind if I make a couple of stops?" Jeremiah asked. "They're on the way to the Penners'."

"That's fine."

After pulling through the teller window at the bank and dropping off some mail at the post office, Jeremiah turned to Abe. "Why don't you bring some of this fruit to the Penners? I can't eat it all."

"Are you sure you don't mind? I gave it to you."

"Take it. It's the least I can do for someone who's going to all this trouble to help me win favor with the people I never should have left."

"Ya, that would be good then. Mrs. Penner can certainly use some of it in her cooking."

"Now I have a favor to ask of you," Jeremiah said. "Would you mind talking to Mary for me? I want to apologize, but I doubt she'll even give me the time of day."

"You're right," Abe said. "And I can't say I blame her. Good thing I'm not a fighting man, or you would have had your face rearranged."

Jeremiah let out an embarrassed chuckle. "I knew that, which was one of the reasons I was so brave."

"Not so brave," Abe corrected.

"You got that right. More like stupid."

Jeremiah drove toward the Penners' house, but Abe asked

him to stop a half block away. "I don't want to alarm Mary before I have a chance to talk to her."

"Good idea." Jeremiah pulled up to the curb. "There's a bag in the backseat. We can transfer some of the fruit to that for me, and you can take the box with the rest of it to the Penners."

After Jeremiah pulled away from the curb, Abe stood with his hands on his hips for a moment as he considered how he'd bring up the subject of Jeremiah. It wouldn't be easy after some of the comments Jeremiah had shouted from his car.

Finally, Abe lifted the box and went to the Penners' front door. Before he had a chance to knock, Joseph came around from the back of the house and called out his name.

"Abe, I'm glad you could make it. Sarah was happy when I told her you were joining us."

"Good. I don't want to go where I'm not wanted."

Joseph opened the door and walked inside. Abe followed.

Mary appeared, but she wouldn't even glance at Abe. He watched as she scurried around the kitchen, working around her grandmother, filling serving bowls and setting them on the table.

Joseph came up beside him. "Let's go outside for a moment, Abe."

Abe followed the older man out the back door and into the yard. "Nice garden."

"Ya, but that's not what I wanted to talk to you about. It's Mary. I don't have any idea what's gotten into her. She's acting very strange."

"I think there are quite a few things about Mary that we may never understand."

"I know." Joseph kicked his toe on the ground. "It's difficult watching her deal with her problems. I wish I could fix everything for her."

"That most likely wouldn't be good. Mary needs to learn how to fix her own problems."

Joseph pursed his lips and nodded. "I'm sure you're right. Just don't let her mood tonight bother you."

"Trust me," Abe said. "I've seen her in much worse moods than this."

"Why do you bother with her, Abe?" Joseph narrowed his eyes and gave Abe a piercing stare. "There are plenty of young women who would be happy to be courted by you."

Abe chuckled. "I'm not so sure about that, but even if that's the case, I've always had a soft spot for Mary."

Joseph folded his arms, never averting his gaze. "But why? Is it just a physical attraction, or do you really care about her?" Before Abe had a chance to answer, Joseph continued. "Mary is very special, but she's been through more in her short lifetime than many other girls in our community. I don't want her to get hurt. Can you be there for her, even when she doesn't want you there?"

"That's a lot of questions," Abe said.

"Then just answer the first one. Why do you have a soft spot for Mary?"

"I sure wish I could tell you. I've often wondered that myself. Sometimes I lie awake at night thinking about all the things she says and does, and I try to come up with reasons to move on and look for someone else. But when I wake up the next morning, I'm that much more determined to do whatever it takes to make Mary trust me."

"She trusts you as much as she has ever trusted anyone. And I think she might even love you, Abe." Joseph relaxed his position slightly.

"Love me? I doubt that."

Joseph chuckled. "She just has a difficult way of showing it. Her grandmother and I suspect she saw some very bad things—worse than we can ever imagine—that still haunt her."

"I'm sure you're right. Mary is a hurting woman, but behind that wall of steel is a sweet woman who loves the Lord." Abe grinned. "Every now and then I catch a glimpse of it, like when she's serving a family in the restaurant or when she speaks of you and Mrs. Penner."

"That's nice to hear," Joseph said as he gestured toward the house. "Let's get back inside before the ladies think we've abandoned them."

"Abe, you sit over there," Mary said as she pointed to her regular chair. "Grandma and I thought it might be better since you have such long legs."

He was surprised she spoke to him after the cold shoulder he'd gotten earlier. "I'll sit wherever you want me to."

"Let's say the blessing now," Joseph said.

They all joined hands and bowed their heads and listened while Joseph thanked the Lord for the blessing of such a beautiful day, having Abe for dinner, and for the food they were about to eat. It was simple but heartfelt.

"So, Abe, how many hired workers do you have on the farm now?" Joseph asked as they passed the food around the table. "I hear you just hired someone new."

Abe explained how David had come to him about his friends needing jobs. "I brought one man on recently—Jonathan—and he seems to be working out just fine. He's worked with his hands before he got his office job, so I just had to teach him some of the basics of farming."

"Think he might stay?"

"I'm not sure. Farming is one of those things you either love or really dislike. After he gets comfortable with what I taught him, I'll have a better idea."

Joseph shook his head. "Too bad so many of our Mennonite boys aren't more interested in farming."

Abe was about to put a forkful of food into his mouth, but he stopped. Was this a good time to risk mentioning

Jeremiah? Silence fell over the table. A few seconds later, Abe decided he might as well mention it now. He had nothing to hide, and Mary would find out eventually. "Jeremiah wants to come work for me."

Mary scowled at Abe. "How can you suddenly become such good friends with such a vile man?"

Her grandfather reached for her hand, but she pulled away. When Joseph turned to Abe, the look of helplessness on the older man's face was evident.

Abe looked directly at Mary. "I hesitated at first, but we've chatted a few times. He wants to come back to the church. I took him over to Franz Bartel's to discuss having him come back to the church today, and Franz thought that was a good idea."

Mary played with the food on her plate, pushing her vegetables around but not eating them. When she looked up at Abe, he saw a flicker of angst. "That man can't be trusted. Aren't you concerned he might do something to sabotage you?" she asked.

Abe shook his head. "Not really, although the thought that he might be using me crossed my mind."

"There is that," Sarah said. "Plus the fact that he has a history of bad behavior might make you think twice."

Joseph looked at his wife. "But, Sarah, through the Lord, Jeremiah can be made a new man. Don't forget about the prodigal son."

"I do think the Lord's timing is an indication of what I'm supposed to do," Abe said. "The farm has expanded, and I need more people. Jeremiah's timing was perfect. I prayed about it when Jeremiah first came to me, and everything seems to be falling into place."

Mary put her fork down and placed both hands in her lap. Her eyes appeared glazed as she stared down at the wall. Her shield had returned. Abe wished he'd waited to discuss this with her first before having a conversation about it with her family, but once again the Lord's timing had kicked in, and he followed what he felt led to do.

"Blessings," Joseph said. "I'll pray that Jeremiah is able to help you with your farm and that he follows the examples the Lord has set before him."

"Thank you," Abe said. He glanced over at Mary, whose body appeared rigid as she moved her gaze to something on the table. When he looked up, he saw that her grandparents had noticed it, too.

Sarah's chair screeched across the floor as she stood. "Anyone ready for dessert?"

Abe rarely skipped the opportunity for something sweet, but at the moment it didn't appeal to him. He stood up and carried his plate to the sink. "No, thank you, Mrs. Penner. I appreciate the delicious meal, but I need to be heading back home. I have an early morning tomorrow."

"I understand," Sarah said softly.

"Excuse me while I go call for"—Abe looked at Mary then at Joseph, who offered a slight smile—"my ride." He went outside and punched in Jeremiah's phone number. "Can you pick me up in a few minutes?" he asked.

"I'll be there in about ten minutes," Jeremiah said.

Abe went back inside and thanked Sarah again for the food. Mary was nowhere in sight, but Joseph offered to walk outside and wait with him.

Once they were on the front lawn, Joseph spoke up. "We need to pray for Mary and her forgiving spirit. This is obviously very difficult for her, but she needs to realize that most people aren't judging her about her past."

"Yes, I know," Abe agreed. "I'll do my best to help her, but I have to admit it will be much easier if she would open up and talk to me about how she feels and what she's thinking. She started to, but something is holding her back."

Joseph shook his head. "I wouldn't count on her ever opening up completely. Mary is a very private young woman."

Jeremiah pulled up at that moment. He waved to Joseph, who waved back. Once Abe was in the car and buckled up, Jeremiah took off toward the farm.

"How'd it go?"

Abe wasn't sure what to tell Jeremiah, but he wasn't going to lie. "I talked about hiring you for the farm."

Jeremiah snorted. "Oh, I bet that went over like a lead balloon." He cleared his throat. "Sorry."

※

No matter how hard Mary tried, she couldn't let go of the pain from her past. She sat on the edge of her bed, staring at the box she'd pulled out of the closet and placed on her bed. Until now she'd avoided it, but all the emotional stirrings had lately brought it to mind. A knock on the door interrupted her thoughts.

"Mary," Grandma said. "Mind if I come in?"

"I don't mind." Mary shifted to face the door as it opened. "Did you need me for something?"

Grandma's stern face softened as she saw the box on the bed. "No, Mary, but I think you need me." She sat down next to Mary and took her hand. They sat in silence for several minutes.

"Grandma, if it weren't for Mama getting pregnant with me, do you think she'd still be here?"

Her grandmother's chin quivered before she lifted her head and looked directly at Mary. "We cannot do that, Mary. Going back and trying to figure out what might have been will only weaken and eventually destroy our faith."

"But if Mama hadn't gotten pregnant, you wouldn't have told her to leave."

A flash of confusion flickered through Grandma's eyes. "Is that what you think? That I told your mama to leave?"

Mary hung her head and slowly nodded. "Isn't that what happened?"

"No, not at all." Grandma's eyes glistened with tears, but she reached out and gently stroked the side of Mary's face with the back of her hand. "When she admitted what she'd done, we were very upset. I said some things that upset her. . .things I shouldn't have said, but I never told her she had to leave. In fact, I told her she couldn't leave. She had to stay home."

"But—"

Grandma lifted a finger to shush Mary. "We told her that as long as she lived in our home, she was to follow our rules. She told us our rules were archaic, and she stormed out." Grandma allowed a tear to escape. "That was the last time we saw her."

Grandma's version of what happened was quite different from Mama's, but Mary knew how time altered things. Even some of her own memories had blurred.

"Mary?"

Mary glanced up. "I don't know what to do now. . .or what to think."

"Why don't you go ahead and open the box? There might be something in there that can help you through this time." Grandma brushed a tear from her cheek. "And if there's not, I'll be here for you, no matter what."

"It just doesn't seem right," Mary said softly. "Mama isn't here anymore, so what's the point?"

"She obviously wanted you to have whatever it is. If it were me. . ." Grandma's voice trailed off as she turned back to look at the box. "But it's not me."

Mary took a chance and studied her grandmother's face. The pain she saw was as intense as the ache in her own heart. For the first time, she considered what the impact of her mother's actions had on Grandma. She had to fight the tears to keep them from falling, but a couple still escaped. Now she realized that the box she'd kept in her closet meant as much to her grandmother as it did her.

"Mary, you're a grown woman now. It is time to deal with your past."

Grandma was right. Mary nodded. "Yes, you're right." She paused.

"Would you like me to open it?" Grandma asked.

Mary stood, swallowed hard, and shook her head. "No, I think I can do it now."

"Do you want me to leave?" Grandma's quavering voice shook Mary even more.

"Please stay." Mary lifted the box and turned around to face Grandma, whose gaze locked with hers. "Let's open it together."

The box was sealed tightly with packing tape. Mary picked at one end of the tape while her grandmother snagged the other. They pulled at the same time, releasing the flaps that had been shut for many years.

Grandma stilled Mary's hand. "Let's pray about this before we look."

Mary nodded and squeezed her eyes shut. As Grandma prayed for the emotional strength and understanding of the meaning behind whatever Elizabeth had placed in this box, tears managed to stream their way down Mary's cheeks. When they both said "Amen," Mary opened her eyes and saw that Grandma's eyes were misty.

"Ready?" Grandma asked.

Mary opened one flap, and Grandma lifted the other. Grandma gasped as the plain white kapp came into full view.

"It's Elizabeth's kapp—the last one she wore before she. . .before she left." She pointed to some initials on the back. "Your mother always liked to monogram her kapps, and this time she used green thread because she ran out of brown."

Mary leaned over the box to see if there was anything else inside. There was—a sealed envelope with her name on it. She pulled it out, turned it over, and cleared her throat.

"Go on, Mary," Grandma urged as she hugged the kapp to her chest. "Open it."

Mary fumbled with the envelope flap until she finally ripped it open. She pulled out a brief letter addressed to her.

"Read it to yourself first," Grandma said. "Then if you don't mind my reading it, I will."

"I'd like to read it aloud the first time if you don't mind."

Grandma glanced down, sniffled, then looked back at Mary, nodding. "If that's what you want to do."

"It is." Mary lifted the letter and studied it for a few seconds before she began.

My dearest Mary,

I want you to know how much I love you. Your life hasn't been easy, and it's my fault. I am terribly sorry for all I've put you through, but I never knew what to do.

When I was sixteen, I was very foolish, and I left the church for a life that seemed very exciting. And it was for a while. But then you came along, and I didn't know the first thing about how to raise a child. All I knew was that I longed for my old, simple life, but instead of going back and begging for forgiveness, I let my pride take control, and I tried to follow the ways of the world.

I've kept my kapp as a symbol of who I used to be and what I still wish I could be. However, the mistakes I've made have snowballed out of control. If you are reading this, I'm probably not in this world any longer. However, I want you to know that I've never stopped praying, so perhaps the Lord will have mercy on me and allow me into His kingdom.

All the things I told you about Grandma and Grandpa are true, but they're the truth from a rebellious teenager's rationalization. Now that I'm an adult with my own daughter, those truths are somewhat blurry. I wish I had been a better mother and found a way to bring you back to where I came from—back to a safer place where you'd be protected and surrounded by love. But I was scared. I never want you to have the fears I faced all my adult life, so please study your Bible and listen to your grandparents, whom I am sure will welcome you with the love of Jesus and love you as much as I do.

Trust me, dearest Mary, when I say I wanted to take you home, but the shame I felt kept me away. Tell your grandparents how much I cared about them and appreciated all the love they gave me. Your grandfather tried numerous times to contact me in the early days after I left, but I was too stubborn to accept his calls. Even my Yankee friends begged me to return home, so I pushed them out of my life as well. When you were much younger, asking questions about family, my words were only half truths. I left out the part about God's grace and mercy as it came through my parents—your grandparents. Until I had you, I never understood my own mother, but after I was faced with so much responsibility, I realized what she did was out of love.

Please keep this kapp as a symbol of who I wish I was and know that I loved you with all my heart. Pray every day and never turn your back on your Creator.

Love,
Mama

A flood of unfamiliar emotions washed over Mary as she looked up into Grandma's stunned eyes. They remained transfixed until Grandma's shoulders began to shake as tears rolled down her cheeks.

eleven

Jeremiah pulled the car up to the front of Abe's house. "I hope I don't blow things for you with Mary."

Abe opened the car door but remained sitting. "Mary is a very complex woman. Until recently I thought we might be making progress in our relationship, but there's something about her I can't figure out."

"You might never figure it out."

"Maybe you're right, brother."

"Women."

"Ya." A flurry of emotions swarmed through Abe. "I care about her too much to forget about her, but I've reconsidered trying to make her my wife."

"Wife? Dude. That's serious."

"You're right. It's very serious. But when the Lord calls me to do something, I know I'm supposed to submit to His ways. I have to admit, lately I haven't been sure what He wants me to do."

"I'm probably not the one to tell you this, Abe, but you might be overthinking your relationship and trying too hard with Mary. Even if she is the one for you, try just letting things happen."

Abe swung his legs out, then stood. "Thanks for the ride, Jeremiah. I'll see you soon."

"Hey man, I appreciate all this time you're spending with me, but don't risk your relationship with Mary just for me."

Abe bent over to look at Jeremiah. "If doing the Lord's calling and helping you get back into the church hurts my relationship with Mary, it's clear the relationship isn't right for me." He started to turn and walk inside, but he stopped. "Oh, and Jeremiah, you need to apologize to Mary soon."

"I will." Jeremiah smiled and lifted his hand in a wave. "See ya, Abe."

After Jeremiah pulled away from the house, Abe went inside and looked around at the sparse furnishings. His mother's feminine touch had long since been replaced by utilitarian design. Everything in the house had a purpose. It was all easy to maintain.

But it seemed so empty—like Abe's heart.

He rinsed his coffee mug from earlier before walking back to his bedroom, where he got ready for bed. The sheets were slightly cooler than the air that had already started getting muggy from the humid Florida heat. He pulled the blanket off and slid beneath the top sheet. As his eyes closed for his evening prayer, images of Mary flitted through his mind.

He thought about how the softness of her face weakened his knees when they were together, but the abrupt changes frightened him. He thought about Jeremiah's words. Had he been trying too hard? Had he assumed the Lord's intentions for him and Mary, just because he'd always had those feelings for her? Feelings like that were temporary while the Lord's plan was eternal.

As Abe prayed for guidance, he tried to push everything else from his mind. His upbringing had taught him to rely on the Lord and not his own desires. Now he needed to follow the path God set before him.

It had been a long day full of emotional highs and lows, creating an exhaustion that was stronger than any physical tiredness Abe had ever experienced. As sleep came, he kept his thoughts on the Lord.

❧

Mary awoke the next morning feeling like a weight had been lifted off her. Her mother's kapp lay on her otherwise bare dresser. She got out of bed, walked over to the dresser, and stared down at the pristine white kapp that would forever remain a symbol of her mother's desire to return to her faith.

After Mama's death, Mary realized that all this time she had blamed herself and Grandma for everything. If it weren't for her, Mama would still be alive and living in the faith she'd grown up with. Now, after hearing Grandma's side of the story, she wasn't sure about anything. It was so easy to blame Grandma for Mama having to struggle so hard, but Mary remembered the stubborn streak that had been the main source of conflict between her and her mother. Mary suspected Grandma's words held a stronger ring of truth than Mama's version.

After dressing, Mary went into the kitchen, where Grandma stood in front of the stove frying bacon. "I thought you might be hungry," she said. "You didn't eat much of your supper last night."

Mary still wasn't all that hungry, but she didn't tell Grandma. Instead she poured herself a cup of coffee and asked what she could do to help.

"Nothing. I told your grandpa you might be a little late this morning."

"Why would I be late?"

Grandma shook her head. "I wasn't sure how you'd feel after last night."

The soft side of her grandmother was disconcerting to Mary. She'd grown used to her sternness, but she'd seen Grandma smile more, show sorrow through tears, and express her feelings, all in the last few days. Maybe those sides of Grandma were there before, but Mary chose not to notice. That revelation hit Mary hard.

"Grandma," Mary began, "you and Grandpa have been very good to me. I want you to know how much I appreciate everything."

"We love you, Mary." Grandma didn't look up from the pan as she dabbed at her cheek with her sleeve. "After your mama left, we felt as though the sun would never shine on our house again. People from the church talked to us and assured us that the Lord was watching over your mother, but we doubted that."

"I think the Lord understands. What you went through must have been terrible."

"It was."

"Mama was good to me," Mary said, hoping to comfort Grandma—at least a little. "She didn't always know what to do, but she let me know she loved me."

Grandma swiped at her cheek with her sleeve. "This will be the first time I ever said this aloud, but during that time, we let our grief swallow up our faith."

"I understand, and I'm sure the Lord does, too."

"Ya, He is much wiser than any of us will ever be. For that I am grateful. And I'm thankful He brought you home to us. Your mama might have conceived you in sin, but you've turned out to be a precious child of the Lord."

When Grandma handed Mary a plate filled with bacon and eggs, Mary looked at it. "I'll eat as much as I can, but this is a lot of food."

"Don't go to work hungry."

Grandma sat down with her mug of coffee. "I know this is difficult for you, but it's time we talked about something."

Mary put down her fork. "About Mama?"

"Neh, this is about Jeremiah. He has asked Abe to pray with him. Abe told us that Jeremiah said some things to you that were upsetting."

Mary tried to hide her feelings, but she knew Grandma could see right through her steely expression. "Do you believe Jeremiah?"

"It's not up to me to believe him, but I do know that God

is forgiving. If Jeremiah is sincerely repentant, the Lord will welcome him back into His fold." Grandma reached for Mary's hand that had stilled on the table. "Just like He would have welcomed back your mama."

Grandma's point hit hard. "It's not easy," Mary said.

"I know. It's never easy for us, but we have to hold on to our faith and trust Him. As long as we're right with the Lord, His plan, which is greater than anything we might want, will prevail."

After breakfast, Mary washed her plate and left for the restaurant. Grandma had some shopping to do, and she said she wouldn't be able to get there until right before the lunch rush.

Shelley was gathering an armload of plates when Mary arrived. "Oh good. You're just in time to give me a hand with these." She nodded toward a couple of plates on the counter. "If you don't mind."

"Of course." Mary pulled a clean apron from a hanger, slipped it on, and tied it before lifting the plates. "I'm right behind you."

Once Shelley's customers were served, Grandpa asked Mary to help finish up with the biscuits before taking over her station in the dining room. She was used to the chaos, and today she was happy she didn't have time to think. That would come later.

Mary had just finished rolling and cutting the last pan of biscuits when Grandpa came back to the kitchen. "There's a strange man out there asking about you."

"A strange man? What did he ask?"

Grandpa lifted his hands. "He wanted to know if I knew Mary Penner. I told him you were my granddaughter."

"Did you ask his name?"

"Ya. He gave me this." Grandpa pulled a slip of paper from his pocket. "Jimbo." He tilted his head in confusion. "Do you know anyone by that name?"

Mary's heart thudded. The only Jimbo she knew was Jim Jr., son of Big Jim, the man who owned the bar where Mama had worked. She had only a few vague memories of Jimbo, who was about four or five years older than her.

The first time she saw him was when Mama had just gotten the job working for his dad. He had a foul mouth, and he told her his dad was the most important person in town— that she needed to be nice to him or her mother wouldn't have a job. Another time he'd pressed her against a wall and touched her in places that made her cringe. She managed to get away, but he told her if she ever mentioned it, he'd make sure her mother was fired. Mary managed to avoid him after that, except the few times he'd been in the bar when Mary went with her mother to pick up her paycheck. And that night when his dad, Big Jim, had given her the bus ticket to Sarasota.

"Mary?" Grandpa asked softly as he placed his hand on her arm. "Do you want to go see what he wants?"

"No," she said. She had to grab hold of the counter for balance as her awful memories threw off her equilibrium.

"Who is he?"

Mary pulled her lips between her teeth as she tried to find a way to let Grandpa know without going into too much detail. Finally she blurted, "He's the son of Mama's old boss."

Grandpa's forehead crinkled. "Then why don't you want to see him? Did he do something to hurt you?"

Shame prevented her from telling everything. "He's just not a very nice man."

"That was a long time ago, Mary. Maybe he's changed."

She doubted it, but she'd seen much stranger things. Her thoughts flew back to her mother's kapp on her dresser. "Maybe."

Grandpa frowned and shook his head. "If he's dangerous,

I don't want you talking to him yet."

Shelley charged through the doorway. "It's a zoo out there. Looks like tourist season has hit hard this year." She clipped her order to the board. "Are you almost finished with the biscuits, Mary?"

"I'll be out there in a minute," Mary said. After Shelley went back out to take more orders, Mary turned to face Grandpa. "Where is he sitting?"

"Over in the front corner by the window." He paused then strode toward the door. "I'll have Shelley wait on him. You take the other side."

"Thank you."

After Grandpa left the kitchen, Mary bowed her head. *Lord, give me the wisdom and strength to handle whatever is about to happen.* She opened her eyes then shut them again. *I pray that nothing happens.*

Mary sucked in a deep breath, squared her shoulders, and marched out into the dining room. She tried hard not to look at the man she wanted to forget.

The crowded restaurant was a blessing for Mary. All the tables between her and Jimbo were filled, and a couple of tall customers blocked her view from most angles. But still, his presence loomed and brought a sense of foreboding.

Mary scurried around the dining room, trying to focus on her customers, but the one time she allowed a glimpse in Jimbo's direction, she caught him staring at her. Her mouth went dry. He hadn't changed much—just a few extra pounds, a few lines on his face, and some stubble on his chin. He had the same sinister look in his eyes that had always given her a creepy feeling.

Grandpa caught up with Mary in the kitchen. "I see him watching you."

Mary shuddered. "I can only imagine what he wants."

"I'll go talk to him and tell him you're too busy."

"I doubt that will matter to Jimbo." Mary snorted. "Mama used to say he would grow up to be a thug, and it looks like she was right."

"You can't judge a man by the way he looks, Granddaughter."

Shelley brushed past Mary. "Some guy out there is determined to talk to you, Mary. Every time I pass him, he asks how much longer." She hesitated a few seconds then added, "Some of the other customers are starting to get annoyed."

Mary pressed her finger to her temple. Jimbo was disrupting business for her grandfather and making Shelley's job more difficult. "I'll talk to him then."

"I'll be right behind you," Grandpa said.

She started to tell him no, she'd deal with it on her own, but a flashback of last night's conversation with Grandma stopped her. "Let's go then."

Mary charged right up to Jimbo's table and stood in front of him, arms folded and feet shoulder-width apart. "What do you want with me, Jimbo?"

He glanced up at her and started cackling. "You are one ridiculous-looking chick, Mary."

"What do you want?" she repeated.

Jimbo's gaze darted behind her, where she suspected her grandfather stood, then he looked back at her. "I don't need an audience."

"Too bad. You came here and said you wanted to talk to me. Now talk."

"Not with the old man staring at me." Jimbo leaned back in his chair and extended his legs across the space between his table and the next one. "I'll just wait right here until we can have a private conversation."

Grandpa stepped up. "Whatever you have to say to my granddaughter, you can say in front of me."

"No offense, Gramps, but this is a private conversation."

Mary turned toward Grandpa and saw his face redden and

his fists clench at his sides. He was obviously infuriated, but his Mennonite faith wouldn't allow him to act on it—at least not with his fists.

"Grandpa," she whispered as she took hold of one of his fists and tugged at him. "Let's leave him alone now. He's obviously just trying to upset us."

"I cannot allow anyone to talk to my granddaughter like this."

"It's just words," Mary said. "C'mon."

Jimbo snorted. "Look at the baby run away with her cowardly grandfather. No wonder your mother couldn't stand it here. What kind of people are you, anyway?"

Anger boiled inside Mary, but her Mennonite teachings popped into her mind. *Lord, please forgive me for these feelings, but I'm only human.* She felt her grandfather resist, so she pulled even harder. "He's just trying to make you do something you'll regret," Mary whispered.

Grandpa's jaw remained tight as he nodded. "You're right."

"I'm not sure how we're going to get him to leave," Mary said on their way back to the kitchen. "Looks like he's determined to make our lives miserable."

They'd barely reached the kitchen door when Grandpa softly said, "I'm calling the police. I can't allow him to threaten you."

"He didn't exactly threaten me," she reminded him. "He just said he wanted to talk to me privately."

"I'm still calling the police." Grandpa pulled his cell phone from his pocket and stepped toward the back door.

Mary glanced across the dining room and spotted Abe and Jeremiah sitting in her station. She felt as though her world was imploding. She wasn't ready for these two very different pieces of her life to meet.

Shelley gently touched Mary's arm. "Is there anything I can do?"

"I don't know," Mary admitted. "I never expected to see anyone from. . ." Her chin quivered, and she sniffled and glanced down.

"You don't have to say anything," Shelley said. "I just want you to know I'm praying for you."

"Thank you," Mary said. She forced a shaky smile. "Isn't it amazing how we seem to be taking turns needing the other one to hold us up?"

Shelley nodded. "That does seem to be the case. I'm glad we have each other."

Mary noticed Shelley's eyes refocusing on something behind her, so she glanced over her shoulder and saw Grandpa approaching. "Did you call the police?"

"Ya." Grandpa looked frustrated. "They said unless there was a blatant threat, they can't really do much. They'll let the patrol officers know, and they'll come out when they get a chance." He cleared his throat. "Something about this not being a high priority."

With as much confidence as she could muster, Mary lifted her head. "I'm sure we'll be just fine. I'm not going to let some mean man from my past make me afraid."

"Would you like to go on home?" Grandpa asked from behind her.

"No, we're too busy. I'll work until the crowd settles."

"Let me know if I need to do anything, okay? I'll keep a close eye on you." Grandpa paused before he gestured toward the dining room. "Oh, one more thing you need to know. Abe's here with Jeremiah."

"Yes, I know," Mary said.

"You okay with that?"

She smiled to ease the angst she saw on Grandpa's face. "Yes, I am just fine."

"You're a strong woman, Mary," Shelley said.

An expression of pride replaced the one of worry on

Grandpa. "That's because she's my granddaughter."

Mary and Shelley both laughed. "I don't know about my personal strength, but I'm fortified with friends and knowing the Lord is with me, no matter what."

"Ya." Grandpa patted her and Shelley on the shoulders. "Now I gotta go see how we're doing on the breads."

Mary stared at the door to the dining room then took a deep breath. "Time to go face the lions."

"You go see what Abe and Jeremiah want. I'll try to deal with that strange man," Shelley said.

After Shelley disappeared into the dining room, Mary went toward Abe and Jeremiah's table. She lifted her order pad and pencil. "Have you decided what you want?"

Abe glared at Jeremiah, who cleared his throat. "Um. . . Mary, I want to. . ." He tossed a helpless look in Abe's direction, but Abe looked away. Mary couldn't help but notice Jeremiah's discomfort.

"You want to what?" she asked.

"Look, Mary, I'm really sorry about those things I said to you that weren't respectful. I was just being. . .well, I was being a jerk."

Mary blinked then turned toward Abe, who nodded. "He means it," Abe said softly.

From the first time they'd met, Jeremiah had never been nice to her. When he'd shouted those comments from the car, Mary was shocked at how crude he could be.

"Please, Mary. I want us to be friends," Jeremiah continued. "I don't think I'll ever be able to make it all up to you, but I'd at least like a fresh start."

The swirl of thoughts in Mary's head nearly made her dizzy. Too much was happening too fast.

Abe glanced up, and his eyes widened. He pointed to something behind Mary. She spun around and found herself face-to-face with Jimbo. Her mouth instantly went dry.

"I told the old man I wanted to talk to you, and I'm not taking no for an answer," Jimbo said as he placed his face inches from hers. "You have something of mine that I want."

Fear welled inside Mary's chest. "You don't know what you're talking about, Jimbo. I don't have anything of yours."

His eyes narrowed, and a smirk covered his lips. "I was there. I saw my dad give you that box."

The box. Mary's mind went back to that day when Big Jim had broken the news and given her the bus ticket and box. Jimbo had been with him.

"What's in that box is not yours," Mary said.

"Oh, but I believe it is. My father gave you something that's rightfully mine. He's gone now, and now I've come to claim it."

Mary was more surprised than frightened. "That box—"

Jimbo didn't give her a chance to finish her statement before grabbing her by the arm so tight she let out a yelp. "You're giving me whatever was in that box my father gave you, and I'm not leaving until I have it."

Before Mary had a chance to react, both Abe and Jeremiah stood. One of the chairs crashed to the floor, sending a startling collective gasp over the guests in the restaurant.

Next thing she knew, Abe was on one side of Jimbo, and Jeremiah was on the other. Abe's large frame towered over Jimbo, and with stocky Jeremiah on the other side, he looked terrified. They each took one of his arms and lifted him off the floor. Mary stood with her mouth gaping open as they walked Jimbo to the door, where they nearly slammed into a pair of uniformed police officers.

twelve

"We got a call to stop by here," one of the officers said. "We were a few streets over. Do you need some assistance?"

Jeremiah looked at Abe and nodded. "Yes, sir, this man threatened one of the women who works here," Abe said.

The officers exchanged a glance before one of them spoke up. "We understood this wasn't a physical threat."

"There wasn't a physical threat when Mr. Penner called, but that has changed. This man grabbed Miss Penner right before you arrived."

The officers both nodded then stepped forward to take over with Jimbo. Abe's muscles were still tight, but he let go. Jimbo kicked one of the officers and tried to flee, but Abe was quick. He caught Jimbo and returned him to the police officers within seconds.

"Sir, you just made one big mistake."

Joseph had made his way over to them by now. "I didn't think we'd see you any time soon," he said to the officers. "Thanks for coming when you did."

One of the officers grinned. "You've been good to us, and we were in the neighborhood."

The men followed the officers outside where they handcuffed Jimbo, read him his rights, and put him in the back of the police cruiser. Joseph, Jeremiah, and Abe each told the officers what had happened. After the officers left, Abe patted Jeremiah on the back. "Thanks for helping out."

"Yes, I want to thank you, too." Mary's soft voice came from behind. Abe and Jeremiah turned to face her, and she looked directly at Jeremiah. "I want you to know that I accept your apology, and I want to apologize to you, too."

Jeremiah smiled and kicked at the ground with his toe. "Thank you, Mary, but you didn't do anything wrong. I'm the one who should do all the apologizing. If I hadn't acted so selfish, we could have been friends." He extracted his hand from his pocket and extended it.

She smiled, took his hand, then turned and met Abe's gaze as Jeremiah let go and stepped back. "Abe, I'm sorry I was so abrupt with you last night," Mary said. "I've been. . .well, out of sorts lately. Can we be friends, too?"

Abe hesitated but eventually nodded. "Ya. I think that's a very good idea, Mary. We can be friends." He felt as though a piece of his heart had been chipped away. He still wanted much more than friendship with Mary, but he'd settle for what she was willing to offer.

"Well, I better get back inside and tend to my customers," Mary said.

Joseph wedged himself between Abe and Jeremiah and put his arms around them. "You fellas want something to eat? My treat."

"Thanks, Mr. Penner. We need to get back to the farm. Jeremiah is starting today."

❧

Mary had been back in the restaurant for nearly an hour when someone from the police department called Grandpa. After he got off the phone, he motioned for Mary to join him in the small office beside the kitchen.

"They have a statement. Apparently Jimbo was very talkative, and they have some information they said you might want to hear."

"Any idea what it is?"

He shook his head. "Neh, but I don't think we'll need to worry about him coming around here anytime soon. He's in jail now, and if he even steps foot on the restaurant property when he gets out, he's going back to jail."

"I wonder why he wanted that box from my mother."

Grandpa cupped her chin. "I'm sure he must have thought it was something it wasn't. I can't imagine a Yankee man wanting a Mennonite woman's kapp. The officer who called asked if we wanted to go to the police station or if it would be better for someone to come here."

"I hope you said they should come here."

"Ya. It's much easier since they have the cars." He pulled her into a hug. "I want to be there with you when they tell you whatever that evil man said."

Her throat swelled with love for Grandpa. "Thank you."

The crowd had died down, so when the police officer arrived to see Mary, they were able to sit at an isolated booth in the corner where no one else could hear. Shelley said she'd seat people as far away as possible for as long as she could. Grandpa brought some mugs and a pot of coffee to the table, and the three of them sat down—the officer, Grandpa, and Mary.

"I'm not sure how much of this is true or how much he made up, but we backed some of it up by calling the police station in Ohio," the officer began. "James McCollum Jr. gave us a statement that we thought would interest you."

"James McCollum Jr.?" Grandpa said.

Mary nodded. "Jimbo."

"Oh." Grandpa turned back to the officer. "Please continue."

"Apparently his father, James McCollum Sr., and your mother were in a relationship. He'd agreed to be involved in a drug sting, and apparently your mother got caught in the crossfire when it fell apart." He paused for a moment when she gasped. "You okay?"

Mary stared at the officer who told her a completely different story from what she'd always believed. She had no idea her mother was in a personal relationship with Big Jim, and she'd thought her mother had been killed because she was an informant. "Please continue."

"James Jr. said he was in the office when his father presented you with the bus ticket and a box. After you left, he asked his father what was in the box, and he was told it was something of great value, but he never said what it was, except it was rightfully his." The officer shifted in his seat. "You wouldn't by any chance still have that box, would you?"

Grandpa's head whipped around to face Mary. "You don't have to—"

She covered his hand with hers. "No, that's okay." Then she looked at the officer. "Yes, I do have the box, and Big Jim was right. It is the most valuable possession I own."

The officer looked extremely uncomfortable as he fidgeted with a sugar packet. Finally he looked at her. "I've been asked to take a look at it if you do so I can let them know what was in it. They think it might be a clue in a case against a drug ring."

Mary grinned. "I doubt that, but I'll be glad to show you what was in it."

Grandpa stood. "Why don't the two of you go on to the house now while we're slow here?"

The officer and Mary left the restaurant and rode in silence. As they pulled up in front of the house, Mary looked around at the place she now called home. It was hard to imagine what her life would have been like if things had been different.

Grandma greeted them at the door, her eyebrows knit in concern. "Come on in. Would you like something to eat, Officer?"

"No, thank you, ma'am. I just want to take a look at the box and let them know what I see."

Mary led the way, with the officer and Grandma bringing up the rear. She knew her grandmother was there to protect her from whatever she might have to deal with.

When they got to her room, Mary pointed to the dresser. "There's the box." She moved her finger to the right, where the kapp lay on top of the note. "And that's what was in it."

He crossed the room and lifted the box. After he turned it upside down and thoroughly inspected it, he focused his attention on the kapp and note. "Mind if I read this?" he asked.

Mary's breath caught in her throat. As difficult as it was, she nodded. "That's fine." She had to turn away to keep from breaking down.

The room grew quiet as the officer read the letter. When he finished, he returned the paper to her dresser and gently placed the kapp back on top of it. "Ms. Penner," he said softly. "I am so sorry about all this. I'll let them know it was only a couple of personal items and nothing of interest that would affect the drug ring case."

Mary had to fight the tears as she nodded her thanks. Grandma put her arm around Mary and pulled her close.

The ride back to the restaurant was as silent as the ride to the house. But when they pulled up at the curb, the officer turned to Mary and handed her a card. "Take care of yourself, Ms. Penner. If anyone ever tries to bother you again, call me."

"I will," she said as she opened her door. "Thank you for being so understanding."

Mary walked back into the restaurant and into Grandpa's arms. "Do you feel like working, granddaughter? If you need—"

"I need to work. This is where I belong."

He let go and gestured toward the kitchen. "Then go get your apron on and get to work."

Mary did as he said. It was already early afternoon, so most of the lunch crowd had left. A few people lingered, and occasionally a group would enter for a late lunch or dessert. Mary was glad for the distraction of work.

She'd finally finished serving the last person on her shift, hung up her apron, and started talking to Shelley when she heard loud voices in the dining room. "I wonder what that's all about?" Shelley asked.

Mary rolled her eyes. "No telling, but after today I think I can handle anything."

Grandpa rushed into the kitchen. "There's been an accident on the Glick farm!"

Her ears rang. With all the turmoil of the day, she'd managed to push Abe to the back of her mind.

Grandpa motioned wildly. "I tried to call Abe's cell phone, and he didn't answer. We need to go see about him."

Mary nodded as her heart raced. "I'm coming with you."

One of Grandpa's regular Yankee customers, Phillip, offered to drive them to the farm. On the way, Grandpa kept asking, "Can't you go faster?"

Mary was glad Phillip remained steady. "No, sir. I'm going the speed limit."

When they pulled onto the road leading to Abe's house, they saw the ambulance. Mary's heart raced even faster. Grandpa took her hand and bowed his head. *Lord, I pray for Your mercy on Abe.*

Phillip pulled the car to a stop beside the ambulance. Mary hopped out and ran to see if Abe was in it.

"Mary," she heard from behind. When she turned around and saw Abe standing there, her knees started to give way. Abe reached out to steady her. "Are you okay?"

She gulped and nodded. "What happened? I thought you were hurt."

"Neh, it was Jonathan Polk's son. He came to help out for a few days, and I hadn't given him the safety talk yet. He went to the old barn and tried to move something. One of the rafters fell down on him, but it looks like he'll be fine. They're taking him to the hospital for x-rays, but they don't think anything is broken."

Abe started to let go of Mary, but she pulled him closer. "Please don't let go. I was so worried something terrible had happened to you, and it scared me, so when Grandpa said he was coming out to check on you, I wanted to come with him, and now I'm—"

"Whoa, Mary, slow down." Abe held her at arm's length and looked in her eyes. "So you were worried about me, huh?"

She nodded and opened her mouth, but nothing would come out.

Abe broke into a grin. "This might sound strange, but I'm glad to know you were worried about me."

Mary pulled back and scowled. "What? You like to worry me?"

"Now that's my Mary. Feisty and direct."

"Why would you want to worry me?"

He caught her off balance as he pulled her back to his chest. "I don't want to worry you, but I'm happy you care enough to check on me."

Mary finally sighed as she thought about how her mother's pride created regrets that could never be overcome. She couldn't make the same mistakes. "Abe?" She looked up into his eyes.

As their gazes locked, her knees went all wobbly again. He steadied her.

"Now I'm worried about you," he whispered. "Would you like to come inside and get something to drink? I'm thinking the heat might be getting to you."

"No, Abe, it's not the heat," she whispered. "It's you."

A grin continued to play at the corners of Abe's lips, but his eyes showed concern. "Are you sure, Mary? I don't want you to get sick."

She closed her eyes and prayed that she wouldn't regret what she was about to say. Then she sucked in a breath and blurted, "Abe Glick, I love you. I've shut you out for so long, I don't know why you even bothered with me."

"You have been a bother," Abe teased. His expression quickly became serious. "But I see something in you, Mary—something that let me know that beneath your shield is a loving, spirited woman."

"So what now?" she asked.

Abe glanced around then took her by the hand. "There are too many people here. Let's go find a private spot so I can show you what now."

Mary's heart raced as she followed Abe to the back of his house. As soon as they were out of sight, he spun her around to face him.

"I've loved you for as long as I can remember—even when we were kids," he said. "I wanted to protect you from everything that might ever hurt you. When I went away to college, thoughts of you helped me through the most difficult times, so the first thing I wanted to do when I returned and saw you again was to make you love me, too."

"Why did you wait a whole year?"

"I didn't want to be in too big of a hurry, and I wanted to make sure everything was just right for us."

"Why did the Lord let me continue being so stubborn?"

"I don't know," Abe replied.

"So what now?"

He let go of her and shoved his hands in his pockets. "The very thing that attracted me to you also scared me. It still scares me. Sometimes you're not easy to approach."

Mary laughed. "So I've heard."

"I wanted everything to be perfect—" Abe glanced around then settled his gaze on her. "But nothing we do can ever be perfect, so. . ."

The look in Abe's eyes melted Mary's heart. When he gently took her hand and tenderly kissed the back of it, her knees turned to jelly. She grabbed hold of Abe's shoulders to keep from falling.

Concern again flickered across his face. "Let's go inside."

"No," she said as she steadied herself. "I like how this is going. I wanna stay and see what happens next."

Abe's laughter was delightful—a sound she knew she'd never get tired of hearing. "Mary Penner, you are so full of surprises."

She jammed the fist of her free hand on her hip and widened her eyes. "So are you, Abe Glick." Then she gestured for him to continue. "Okay, keep going."

He again kissed the back of her hand, never taking his gaze off hers. "Mary, how would you like to live on a farm?"

Mary contorted her mouth and narrowed her eyes. "All depends on what farm we're talking about."

"This farm. With me."

"Hmm." She tapped her chin with her index finger.

Abe placed his hands on her shoulders, his face inches from hers. "Mary Penner, will you make me the happiest man in Florida and be my wife?"

She offered him a teasing look. "Just Florida?"

He grinned as he lifted his arms and gestured wide. "If you say yes, I'll be the happiest man in the world!"

She forced herself not to smile or jump up and down with joy. Instead, she leveled him with as stern a look as she could manage. "What took you so long to ask? Of course I'll be your wife."

"Abe? Mary?"

They glanced up toward the voice. "Grandpa!" Mary gave Abe a quick wink then ran over to her grandfather. "You'll never guess what just happened!"

Grandpa smiled. "Oh, I think I can."

Abe joined them. "I'm sorry, Mr. Penner, I should have spoken to you about this first. With your permission, I would like to marry your granddaughter."

"I'm speaking for Sarah and myself," Grandpa said as he hugged Abe. "You have our full blessing." He turned around to face Mary. "But now we need to get back to town. We have work to do."

Abe waited until Grandpa turned his back before he leaned over for a kiss. "I love you, Mary. You've just made me a very happy man."

"I love you, too, Abe." Mary couldn't believe how easily those words rolled off her tongue.

As the car rolled away from the farm, Mary looked around and thought about how this would soon be her home. Grandpa winked at her and squeezed her hand. The joy between them was so powerful, neither of them had to say a word.

note to the readers:

Shades of the Past is set in the Pinecraft community of Sarasota, Florida, a beach town south of Tampa Bay. Most of the Pinecraft homes are rented by Mennonite and Amish families who have decided to settle in Florida to enjoy the mild winters and white sandy beaches. The houses are small, but they are wired for electricity, which many of the inhabitants enjoy, even if they come from a sect that doesn't typically use electricity.

With Sarasota being a busy beach town, it's difficult to care for large animals, so instead of the traditional horse-and-buggy transportation, most of the Mennonite and Amish residents get around on adult-sized tricycles called bikes or three-wheelers—some motorized and some pedal powered. They attach baskets and boxes to haul larger loads for errands and short trips around the neighborhood, and they use city buses and independent drivers for longer distances.

Some visitors may have a difficult time telling the difference between Amish and the most conservative Mennonites. Most of the Amish women wear kapps with strings, while Mennonite women have a wider variety of head coverings, including crocheted pieces. Mennonite men may have mustaches, while Amish men are likely to only have beards.

Sarasota hosts a variety of Mennonite and Amish orders from other areas, creating a blend of old and new traditions that have evolved during the years. The language tends to be more contemporary than that of some Conservative Mennonite groups.

A few Mennonite and Amish farms still thrive on the outskirts of Sarasota. On most Saturdays, Pinecraft hosts a farmer's market, and roadside stands dot the area on weekdays, with local citrus being the most common produce available.

A Letter To Our Readers

Dear Reader:

In order that we might better contribute to your reading enjoyment, we would appreciate your taking a few minutes to respond to the following questions. We welcome your comments and read each form and letter we receive. When completed, please return to the following:

Fiction Editor
Heartsong Presents
PO Box 719
Uhrichsville, Ohio 44683

1. Did you enjoy reading *Shades of the Past* by Debby Mayne?
   ❏ Very much! I would like to see more books by this author!
   ❏ Moderately. I would have enjoyed it more if

   _____

   _____

   _____

2. Are you a member of **Heartsong Presents**? ❏ Yes ❏ No
   If no, where did you purchase this book? _____

   _____

3. How would you rate, on a scale from 1 (poor) to 5 (superior), the cover design? _____

4. On a scale from 1 (poor) to 10 (superior), please rate the following elements.

   _____ Heroine   _____ Plot
   _____ Hero   _____ Inspirational theme
   _____ Setting   _____ Secondary characters

5. These characters were special because? _____

   _____

   _____

6. How has this book inspired your life? _____

   _____

   _____

7. What settings would you like to see covered in future
   Heartsong Presents books? _____

   _____

   _____

8. What are some inspirational themes you would like to see
   treated in future books? _____

   _____

   _____

9. Would you be interested in reading other **Heartsong
   Presents** titles? ❏ Yes ❏ No

10. Please check your age range:
    ❏ Under 18   ❏ 18-24
    ❏ 25-34   ❏ 35-45
    ❏ 46-55   ❏ Over 55

Name _____

Occupation _____

Address _____

City, State, Zip _____

E-mail _____

the
JOURNEY

Titus Fisher has often made poor choices. When he lived in Pennsylvania, he chose the wrong girl who broke his heart. When he moves to Kentucky, he finally discovers that he possesses woodworking skills. Will he stick with it or return to the old comforts of his life in Lancaster? Suzanne Yoder's talents don't lie in the traditional Amish kitchen, but she suppresses talents that are frowned on by those in her community who believe a woman's place is in the home. Will Titus be impressed or upset when he learns the secrets she hides?

Contemporary, paperback, 384 pages, 5.5" x 8.375"

Heartsong

HEARTSONG PRESENTS TITLES AVAILABLE NOW:

___HP729 *Bay Hideaway*, B. Loughner
___HP730 *With Open Arms*, J. L. Barton
___HP754 *Red Like Crimson*, J. Thompson
___HP758 *Wedded Bliss*, K. Y'Barbo
___HP762 *Photo Op*, L. A. Coleman
___HP785 *If the Dress Fits*, D. Mayne
___HP786 *White as Snow*, J. Thompson
___HP789 *The Bride Wore Coveralls*, D. Ullrick
___HP790 *Garlic and Roses*, G. Martin
___HP806 *Out of the Blue*, J. Thompson
___HP814 *The Preacher Wore a Gun*, J. Livingston
___HP817 *By the Beckoning Sea*, C. G. Page
___HP818 *Buffalo Gal*, M. Connealy
___HP821 *Clueless Cowboy*, M. Connealy
___HP830 *The Bossy Bridegroom*, M. Connealy
___HP834 *Salt Water Taffie*, J. Hanna
___HP838 *For the Love of Books*, D. R. Robinson
___HP850 *Trail to Justice*, S. P. Davis
___HP865 *Always Ready*, S. P. Davis
___HP885 *A Hero for Her Heart*, C. Speare &
          N. Toback
___HP886 *Romance by the Book*, M. Johnson
___HP889 *Special Mission*, D. Mayne
___HP890 *Love's Winding Path*, L. Bliss
___HP893 *Disarming Andi*, E. Goddard
___HP894 *Crossroads Bay*, K. Kovach
___HP897 *Polar Opposites*, S. P. Davis
___HP898 *Parting Secrets*, B. Melby & C. Wienke

___HP901 *Gaining Love*, J. Johnson
___HP902 *White Roses*, S. T. Vannattes
___HP905 *Boxed into Love*, C. Speare &
          N. Toback
___HP906 *Perfect Ways*, J. Odell
___HP909 *Portrait of Love*, D. Mayne
___HP910 *Where the Dogwoods Bloom*, M. Johnson
___HP913 *Exposing Amber*, G. Goddard
___HP914 *Heart of Mine*, L. Bliss
___HP917 *Pure Serendipity*, B. Melby &
          C. Wienke
___HP918 *Fine, Feathered Friend*, K. Kovach
___HP921 *White Doves*, S. T. Vannatter
___HP922 *Maid to Love*, J. Johnson
___HP925 *Mending Fences*, C. Speare & N. Toback
___HP926 *The Thing about Beauty*, D. Robinson
___HP929 *Facing Tessa's Past*, M. Colvin
___HP930 *Wasatch Love*, L. Bliss
___HP933 *Praying for Rayne*, E. Goddard
___HP934 *Lily of the Field*, R. R. Zediker
___HP937 *White Pearls*, S. T. Vannatter
___HP938 *Betting on Love*, J. Johnson
___HP941 *In the Cool of the Evening*, J. Spaeth
___HP942 *Peace, Be Still*, T. Fowler
___HP945 *Perfect Peace*, J. Odell
___HP946 *Redeeming Sarah's Present*, M. Colvin

(If ordering from this page, please remember to include it with the order form.)